Kings Mountain

Kings Mountain

G. CLIFTON WISLER

■ HarperCollins*Publishers*

For Uncle Bob,
who shared my love of history

Kings Mountain
Copyright © 2002 by G. Clifton Wisler
For information address
HarperCollins Children's Books, a division of HarperCollins Publishers,
1350 Avenue of the Americas, New York, NY 10019.
www.harperchildrens.com

Library of Congress Cataloging-in-Publication Data
Wisler, G. Clifton.
Kings Mountain / G. Clifton Wisler.
    p.   cm.
Summary: Fourteen-year-old Frank leaves his mountain home in the South
to help the patriot cause during the Revolutionary War.
ISBN 0-688-17813-8 — ISBN 0-06-623793-9 (lib. bdg.)
1. South Carolina—History—Revolution, 1775–1783—Juvenile fiction.
[1. South Carolina—History—Revolution, 1775–1783—Fiction.   2.
United States—History—Revolution, 1775–1783—Fiction.] I. Title.
PZ7.W78033 Ki 2002   2001039506
[Fic]—dc21

Typography by Larissa Lawrynenko
4 5 6 7 8 9 10
❖
First Edition

The Revolution
in the South

VIRGINIA

• Watauga
Settlements

• Hillsborough

Roan Mtn

• Quaker Meadows

NORTH CAROLINA

Gilbert Town
•

• Charlotte

Cowpens
•

⚔
Kings
Mountain

• Waxhaws

⚔ Battle
of Camden

Wilmington •

Camden •

SOUTH CAROLINA

GEORGIA

Charleston •

ATLANTIC OCEAN

Savannah •

1

*I*N A WAY, IT ALL started with my brother Charlie. He was three years old the spring I was born, but folks say he had already shown the spark of promise. When he was eight, he could run and ride as well as any boy in the Watauga country. He put Pa in mind of himself, Ma told us. As for me, well, I was a different sort altogether. And I don't think I even once measured up to Pa's expectations.

I was just five the summer Charlie tried to ride Mr. Moore's roan stallion. That horse had a temper like no creature I'd ever seen, and it wasn't about to let even a tallish eight-year-old ride it. Charlie got one leg over the roan's back when the horse reared up and threw him hard against the rail fence behind the Moores' barn. My sister, Kate, and I, together with Hope and Josh Moore, saw it. Kate started shouting, but I figured Charlie would hop up and have a second try. I never expected anything so ordinary as a fence rail could kill anybody.

Kate's screams finally set my feet in motion, and I

joined her at the fence. In front of us, Charlie lay as limp as an old rag doll. His eyes were wide open. It was like he'd been surprised by something. A dark gash across his forehead leaked blood.

Mrs. Moore came out and carried Charlie into her parlor, but he was dead by then. Kate and I stood at the fence, stunned. All I could do was stare at the bloodstained ground with my five-year-old eyes and wonder how such a thing could have happened.

"It was God's will," Ma said, but I think Pa faulted Kate and me for allowing it. As if the two of us together could have stopped Charlie from doing whatever was in his mind to do! We buried Charlie on a little hill overlooking the river. Mr. Ed Smith cut Charlie's name in a stone to mark the spot. Afterward, Pa went off into the high country for two weeks. He came back a changed man.

He'd never been the merriest soul on earth, but at least he'd laughed when telling us stories or chasing us through the river. He rarely smiled after Charlie died. On some mornings, he'd sit up on the hill beside the stone and talk to my dead brother. When I did something wrong, you could see right in Pa's eyes that he was thinking how Charlie would have done it better. I was never any good at being the oldest son. In truth, my littler brothers, James and Alexander, were braver and quicker at most everything. They had Pa's yellow hair and blue eyes, too, just like Charlie. My own hair was dark as a raven's wing, and my eyes were big and round as brown marbles. That's how Ma put it anyway.

"You put me in mind of my own ma," she told me more than once. Grandma Hughes had been half-Cherokee, and Ma said I was lucky to have come by her good looks and common sense. I don't think Pa felt that way. When trouble started up with the Indians, most of the neighbors pointed to the resemblance.

"Cherokee Frank," some of them called me. The kind ones, that is. I occasionally overheard a neighbor talking about scalp-takers and baby-killers when I happened by. I glared at them.

"Where would any of them be if the Cherokees hadn't leased them their land?" Ma asked when I told her.

"Ah, they would have gone and stolen it," Kate remarked. "You ought to hear Henry Smith talk. His family got here two years ago, and already they're acting like they own every acre between these mountains and the Mississippi River!"

"Oh?" Ma asked, laughing. "If they've got so much, maybe they can return the skillet they borrowed last winter. And they haven't paid Colonel Carter for the land they're farming."

I frowned to hear Ma so riled. Truth was, people like the Smiths seemed to blow in and out of our valley. Mostly they were looking for cheap land or quick money. They would either move along or discover what Ma called "the secrets of the earth."

"Everything a man or a woman needs, he can find here," Ma had told us a thousand times. "Corn grows tall, and all the animals to feed and clothe us run along the river or walk the woodlands. There's no reason to look to distant peaks or search out greener valleys. This place has all you need."

I understood that by the time I marked my ninth birthday. We planted and harvested the fields along the river, bringing in enough corn for our needs and a little more besides. We watched our cattle and hogs, slaughtering what we required for meat and hides. Pa hunted the hills for wild turkeys and deer. We youngsters fished the river and snared rabbits in the thickets.

Birthdays were special in our family. Ma told me once that Charlie's dying had made her appreciate each year her children walked the earth. But she and Pa had made a fuss over birthdays before, when Charlie was still around. I think it was just her excuse for easing our burdens and having a laugh every once in a while. So when Ma marked off the third day of March on her calendar, she grinned like a hawk that had eyed a plump rabbit sleeping in the grass below.

"Sounds familiar," she said. "Like something important happened once upon a time on this day."

"Ah, Ma, you're joking," my five-year-old brother Alek said. "It's Frank's birthday."

"Sure, you'd remember that," Jamie, who was two years older, added. "You know you sent off—"

A stern glance from Ma hushed Jamie short of giving away whatever secret he was about to blurt out. Kate, who'd turned eleven the month before, herded my brothers outside, and Ma was left to concentrate her gaze on me. I knew she was going to say something about Pa. He'd left a few weeks earlier on a trip to trade fox and rabbit pelts at Camden, the little market town to the east where Grandma Livingstone ran a small tavern.

"Your father expected to be back by now," she told me.

"You can never tell what the weather's like on the other side of the mountains," I said, frowning. "Guess it slowed him down."

"Possibly," she said. "Doesn't mean he isn't thinking about you, Francis. Being here with you today's important. He might make it yet."

He didn't, though. We ate a plump goose that Ma fixed special. She presented me with a Bible that had belonged to her pa, the Reverend Hughes. It was my very first book, and it surprised me to see Pa had neatly lettered my name inside. *Francis Hugh Livingstone*, it read. There were a lot of other names written below, of grandparents and uncles and cousins.

"To remind you that you're part of many others," Ma explained. "A man's never alone who's got family."

I noticed there weren't any Cherokee names in the Bible, and I asked her about it.

"I wouldn't know how to write those names," she told me. "Besides, Cherokees hold their relatives in their hearts. No need reminding you about them."

I nodded, but I didn't understand how both the things she'd said could be true.

Pa returned home two days later. He looked worn and weary, but he managed a rare smile for me.

"You had some trouble, Pa," I said, noticing a bruise on his left forearm.

"Was in a bit of a hurry," he explained. "Traveling by night. Not the smartest thing to do, I know, but there was so much rain. The runoff swelled the rivers and kept me waiting to cross each one. I almost made it back on time."

"Well, it was close enough," I told him as I helped carry bundles inside.

"You can prepare for most things, son, but not all of them," he observed. "The world is mostly trouble, you see. You're of an age to know that, Francis. And of an age to learn what's to be done."

"I'm just nine, Pa," I pointed out.

"That's older'n some ever get to be," he said, glancing over his shoulder toward the little hill where Charlie was buried. He then pulled out a long, rolled buffalo hide. Inside was a rifle.

"Well?" he asked. "Don't you think you ought to look your gun over? Can hardly see it from there."

"It's for me?" I said, refusing to believe my ears.

"A Watauga man needs a good rifle," he explained. "When a Livingstone gets his name written in the Bible, it's time he stands with the men."

"Yes, sir," I agreed.

We celebrated my birthday a second time that night. Ma roasted another goose, and we ate ourselves fat. Pa got out his fiddle, and we sang and danced awhile. Then he presented me with my rifle, together with some drawing pencils and two boxes of paper that Grandma Livingstone had sent along. My uncle Hugh had sent a mouth organ from his farm in North Carolina.

It was the rifle that made that birthday memorable. Ma would probably have been disappointed to hear me say that. But to a boy, a rifle's a special thing. Mine was truly beautiful, too. Crafted by Mr. Jacob Dickert of Lancaster, Pennsylvania, it was long and wonderfully balanced. The stock was polished maple—so shiny you could almost see yourself in its gleam. Near four feet long, stock and barrel, it could hit its mark at well past a hundred yards. It took some practice loading, and the grooved barrel could foul with powder if you didn't keep it clean. But it did deadly work in the hands of a marksman like Pa.

I was rightly proud to own so fine a gun, and I carved my initials in the stock. I oiled the scarred wood, and soon the *FL* seemed as much a part of the weapon as its barrel.

my Dickert

"Takes more than scratching letters to earn a rifle," Pa told me. "A man must learn the use of his tools." He began my lessons early the following morning.

My Dickert soon smelled of sulfur and lead from the practice rounds I fired into a fallen oak under Pa's watchful eye. Lead being hard to come by, we'd dug the balls out of the oak afterward. "You can hit what you aim for," Pa finally declared. "Now it's time to put that skill to use."

I remember that hunt as if it were yesterday. Traces of snow still clung to the peaks, and a chill cut through my buckskin hunting shirt and inched its way between my ribs. To my way of thinking, the morning would have been better spent huddled beside the fireplace with my sister and brothers, doing ciphers on my slate. But I was nine years old, and there was no putting off responsibility.

Most boys looked forward to that sort of day, and in a way, I was no different. But whenever Pa and I set off by ourselves, Charlie's ghost came along. When Pa handed over my rifle, I suspected he was thinking that it should have been Charlie there, how my brother would have learned the loading and cleaning in half the time, that Charlie surely would have hit his mark on the first try.

"Go along ahead," Pa said. I nodded solemnly. As I wove my way through the thickets beyond the river, I remembered all the times I'd walked that same country with Ma's cousin Tsula. That was Cherokee for "fox." Tsula knew all about the woods. He was only ten when I was born and wasn't so much older that he had no time to pass with a younger cousin.

"I enjoy our walks," Tsula told me. "You understand the need to walk softly, to get along with all creatures. These newcomers take more than they need, and they look at others with angry eyes. That's not our way."

By "our way," he meant the Cherokee way.

"You understand what it means to listen to the wind and hear the streams sing," Tsula said. "You're one of us."

But with the Watauga country filling with settlers, being Cherokee didn't win you friends. Pa wouldn't abide me talking about my Indian cousins and the way they lived. And he wouldn't have liked it if he knew that was on my mind that morning.

"Can't two peoples own anything," he grumbled. "So long as there's land out here without anyone on it, people are going to come looking to build themselves a future."

I could read the pain in Ma's eyes when he talked like that. We rarely saw her Cherokee relatives anymore. When we did, they carried rifles and were wary of our neighbors.

"We probably won't walk these woods together again," Tsula had told me finally. "I'm going to make my home farther south, away from the white settlements."

I missed him, but Pa was mostly glad he didn't have to explain Ma's family to new neighbors.

That morning, leading the way into the tall pines of the forest, I remembered how Tsula had said all creatures have a place in the great web of life. Even the smallest insect is there for a reason. I knew Pa had in mind that we find a deer to shoot. He would work the hide into new trousers for my brothers, and we would eat the meat. Ma would make use of most other parts for this and that. In the web, it would be that deer's fate to serve our needs.

I understood that. It wasn't the first time I'd hunted. Tsula had taught me to kill quail with well-aimed rocks. I'd snared plenty of rabbits and caught many fish. Still, I wasn't prepared for the deer.

Pa located the tracks, and we circled around to get

upwind. There were two of them. The buck was considerably bigger, and Pa motioned to mark him as my target. After loading my rifle, I found an opening in the trees and knelt on one knee. The big Dickert felt unusually heavy in my short arms, but I cocked the hammer and took aim. In front of me the buck froze. His eyes turned until they found me. We stared at each other, and I hesitated. He was a beautiful creature, tall and proud, and I couldn't find it in my heart to kill him.

"Shoot," Pa urged. "Fool boy, take the shot."

I took a deep breath, held it a moment, and let it go. Part of me wanted that buck to flee, to scamper off into the thickets and escape.

"Francis," Pa whispered, "what are you waiting for?"

That was when I realized I was waiting for Pa to shoot the deer, for him to do the hard things the way he always had. I swallowed, silently asked the buck's forgiveness, and squeezed the trigger. Flint ignited powder, and the Dickert spit its deadly pellet in a storm of smoke and fire. The recoil jarred my shoulder. The air clouded, and I spit the taste of sulfur from my mouth.

"Good work," Pa said, slapping my shoulder. When the smoke cleared, I stared at the fallen buck as the doe raced away.

"It was such a beautiful creature," I told Pa.

"It will feed your family," Pa replied. "It's not doing the easy things that makes you a man. It's doing what's necessary."

I didn't feel a bit older or wiser, though.

We skinned the buck and then began butchering the carcass. We would have fresh meat for dinner. Ma would smoke the rest for eating later, when we were busy planting and had few moments to spare for hunting deer. We left little but bone behind when we finally started home.

That night I sat beside the fireplace, sketching my memory of the buck on a sheet of my birthday paper.

"You do honor to him," Ma said, studying the simple drawing. "Look at how you've captured his eyes! I had an uncle who could make pictures come alive like that. He painted skins. I helped him make the dyes. Soon the flowers will come again. I'll show you how to make the colors. Maybe you've inherited the gift."

"Maybe," I said, adding a bit of shadow with my pencil. "I just draw what I see."

"More than that," she observed. "You draw what you feel."

I supposed that was true. If I had known then what the gift would lead to, I might have set my pencil aside and never lifted it again. But no boy of nine can know what will happen years later. Instead, I finished the drawing and set it beside the bed I shared with my little brothers. Then I took my Dickert rifle from its place beside the cabin's front window and began cleaning the barrel.

"A man takes care of his tools," Pa had told me. I swabbed out the accumulated powder and polished the stock. It was as shiny as the day Jacob Dickert had made it. No one save me would have guessed at the deadly work it had done that morning. Or the deadlier work that lay ahead.

2

YCAMORE SHOALS was an old crossing point and gathering place on the Watauga River. It was only a few miles upstream from our farm, and I'd been there a dozen times before I turned nine. A few days after I shot my first deer, Pa announced that we would go there for a powwow with Ma's people, the Cherokees.

The previous autumn, the Shawnees under Chief Cornstalk had started raiding settlements farther north, and Pa had joined a militia company to fight them. There had been a battle in October, and the Shawnees had signed an agreement, giving up their lands south of the Ohio River. Ma had laughed at the news because the Cherokees claimed the territory themselves. That hadn't stopped settlers from pouring into what they called Kentucky. The powwow was an effort to settle the question without another fight.

For me, it was like another birthday gift. Tsula came, bringing his wife and little daughter. Ma saw uncles and cousins she hadn't visited in years. We joined in singing and dancing and celebrating. I even won a footrace against two cousins and Josh Moore, who was a whole year older.

After eating and enjoying ourselves, it was time to "talk turkey," as Pa put it. The leaders of the white settlers sat down with the Cherokee chiefs and agreed to terms. The deal had nothing to do with the Watauga lands. Ma had our farm as a gift from her Cherokee grandmother, and our neighbors leased their land. After the treaty signing, John Sevier and James Robertson bought the leased country for trade goods valued at two thousand English pounds. That was a fair amount of money by Pa's figuring, but the sale didn't make everyone happy.

"You shouldn't smile about what's happened here," Tsula told me when we walked along the river. "Tsugunsini is angry. He says the old men have sold away our future. Many young men listen to him. There will be trouble because of this."

Tsugunsini, called Dragging Canoe by white people, made a speech before leaving. I knew only a few Cherokee words, and Dragging Canoe spoke rapidly. I understood the tone, though, and the last part. He intended to keep the Watauga country no matter what treaties were signed.

"It's a bad bargain when you create enemies," Ma declared.

"You can't satisfy everybody," Pa argued. "Some of our people believe we should have just taken the land. Some of the Cherokees believe there should never have been a sale. Everybody just wasn't going to be happy no matter what!"

A month later, in April, fighting started up in Massachusetts. British soldiers fired on the local militia, and an army of farmers marched down and surrounded Boston. That seemed a world away from our peaceful valley, but Pa took on a dark look when he learned of it.

"King George will get around to us," he warned.

Of course, there was never any real question about what side we would be on. Years before, the king had outlawed settlement west of the Appalachian Mountains. We had little use for him, his governors, or his regiments of soldiers. We got by on our own, didn't we? We'd drawn up our own laws, and we saw to it they were kept. If Shawnees started raiding our neighbors, we mustered the militia and went up to help. By the time any British general even found out about trouble, it was usually over.

"But do you consider yourself a rebel, John?" Mr. Moore asked Pa.

"I don't see much difference between being called an outlaw or a rebel," Pa told us. "If King George can spare the army to come out here and cause trouble, we'll give him as much fight as he wants!"

As for the war that was going on up north, we left it to the people living there. The Carolinas were another matter. When thousands of settlers who sided with the king gathered near the mouth of the Cape Fear River that next February, my uncle Hugh and cousin John were among the militia that won the first battle of sorts fought in the southern colonies at Moore's Creek Bridge. The Tories, as the people who remained loyal to King George III were called, were stopped cold. Many were killed. Others lost the urge to defend the king. They set aside their weapons.

There was little time to celebrate, though. A British fleet was on its way with an army determined to capture Charleston. A call for help arrived, and a dozen of our neighbors marched off to support the rebels on the coast. While manning a cannon in a little fort on Sullivans Island, old Jake Grisby claimed to have fired the shot that struck the British flagship.

"Blew that admiral's trousers off his backside," Jake claimed.

We didn't much believe it, but he had a piece of a Charleston newspaper with him. It told all about how Col. William Moultrie's little fort had stood off a whole fleet of ships. The battered admiral and his ships had gone to New York, leaving Charleston in the hands of the rebels.

With no army of redcoats to regain control of his southern colonies, King George enlisted the aid of our enemies. Powder, lead, and muskets that might have been used by Tories went instead to Indians agreeing to raid the western settlements. Dragging Canoe was only one of the willing men the king's agents found.

In July, as representatives of the various colonies met in Philadelphia to decide whether or not to declare us independent of the king's authority, Dragging Canoe led a raid against one of the settlements to the west. Cherokees burned cabins and killed settlers. Terrible stories of suffering made their way to the Watauga, and every man for miles around appeared at the Sunday muster. For defense, the men erected a stockade near Sycamore Shoals. They named it Fort Caswell, after Gen. Richard Caswell, who had commanded the patriots at Moore's Creek Bridge. We were told to pack up and head for the safety of its walls if Indians appeared.

Ft. Caswell

The news of Cherokee raids rested heavily on Ma. I had never seen her so tormented.

"To think that our own people could do such things," she told me. "It breaks my heart."

For me, it wasn't a matter of my heart getting broken. I had stones hurled my way, and once a couple of bigger boys from down the river caught me fishing with my brothers.

"There he is!" one of them shouted. "Cherokee Frank!"

"Fetch Pa," Jamie told Alek.

"You go, too," I told Jamie. He was only eight and wouldn't be any real help in a fight. He stuck by me just the same.

"So, you spying on us?" the taller of the boys asked. "Deciding whose cabin to burn next?"

"Why are you coming up here?" Jamie yelled. "We don't even know you!"

"Hush," I growled.

"You let that little baby do your talking?" the second stranger asked.

"I don't generally talk to idlers and fools," I answered. "And I don't tell my brother what to say. He's not too old, but he's smart enough to recognize what's sensible."

"Meaning we're not?" the bigger boy asked.

"You heard what I said," I told him. "If you have any sense, you can figure the meaning. Now, do you want something?"

The two older boys exchanged a glance. Then they grinned. Before I realized what was happening, they had marched up and pulled me away from the river.

"Well?" the taller one asked. "You going to fight back or let us whip you raw as you lie there?"

I rolled away and got to my feet. Jamie rushed to my side, but I pushed him clear. I would have welcomed Charlie about then, but all Jamie was going to do was get hurt. Besides, Tsula had taught me a trick or two. As the older boys tried to decide which one was going to have the first go at me, I threw myself at the taller one, shoulder first, and knocked the wind out of him. As his companion turned, I knocked his legs out from under him and slammed an elbow across his forehead. That's all I remembered, because once the two of them recovered from my

17

attack, they pounded me into the ground.

Kate appeared half an hour later, red with rage, but the downriver boys had gone. Jamie had a bruise on one arm and a bloody nose. My right eye was swollen shut, and my left shoulder was out of its socket. I had more scrapes and bumps than I could count.

"Should've seen him fight 'em," Jamie boasted. "Took both of 'em, too. They were just too big."

"For a boy who can outrun anyone in the valley, seems pretty foolish to fight two bigger boys," Kate scolded.

"Maybe, but I thought I might surprise them."

"He did," Jamie added.

"Well, I hope they looked worse for it," Kate grumbled. "If not, you might try running next time."

Pa didn't say a word about my scrape. Ma just doctored my cuts and frowned.

"I'll never understand why the stronger ones feel obliged to attack the weaker," she said as she washed the dirt from my forehead. "I'm glad you stood your ground, even though you look to have suffered for it."

I nodded silently. Ma never said much about it, but I knew that I wasn't the only one who was whispered about or called names.

When I next went to the river, Pa handed me my Dickert.

"Never can tell what kind of trouble's apt to come along," he said. "I've heard about unwelcome visitors."

"Sure, Pa," I replied, cradling my rifle. It wasn't loaded, though. I wouldn't shoot at a boy no matter what mean words he had for me. I was only ten, but I knew that much.

We caught two fat catfish that morning, and I looked forward to how they'd taste with a square of Ma's sweet buttered corn bread. I never had the chance to find out, though. Shortly after midday, I heard my name called from a stand of oaks near the river. When I walked over to see who was there, I discovered Tsula waiting.

"I came ahead to tell you," he explained. "A war party is on its way. More than twenty men. Maybe fifty even. Hurry and tell your mother."

"Tsula?" I asked. "You're fighting us?"

"Not me," he said, clasping my hand. "I can never be an enemy of my own family. There are others, though, hungry for war. They're coming."

He was gone as fast as he had come, and I imagined he was off to warn others. I gathered Kate and my brothers and headed for home. By the time we got there, Ma was already piling supplies in the back of a wagon. A smoke plume rose high into the western sky from a few miles downriver.

"They're headed here. Tsula was here," I explained. She nodded somberly and ordered Jamie and me to harness the horses. Kate and Alek helped finish packing the wagon. We met Pa on the way to Fort Caswell.

"Raiders!" Ma shouted. Pa nodded and followed. Dozens of friends and neighbors were already crowding inside the tall stockade by the time we arrived at Fort Caswell. Despite several warnings spread by Cherokee friends, not everyone believed the raiders were coming.

One or two families fled for their lives as a handful of Indians appeared at their cabins. Several women were milking cows when the main party, led by a stern-faced warrior called Old Abram, arrived at the fort. Two managed to reach the gate before we closed it, but Kate Sherill had been off chasing a stray cow. She fled for her life as a tall Cherokee pursued her. Despite her skirts and small stature, Kate managed to keep a step ahead. When she was within a hundred feet of the wall, John Sevier put a rifle ball through the chest of her tormenter. Sevier then reached down and pulled her up over the wall. Kate Sherill's rescue was remembered much better than the two-week fight that followed.

Old Abram's main problem was Fort Caswell. We had a good water supply there and plenty of provisions. Men with rifles stood behind thick wooden walls and fired from cover. Any Cherokee who approached the stockade got shot. We weren't coming out, so to get at us, the whole war party had to charge the wall. Any of them not killed during the charge would be overwhelmed when they tried to force their way up the walls.

The Cherokees tried twice to creep up on the fort in the faint predawn light. Both times, they were discovered. Men ran up to their firing stations and began shooting. Creeping shadows toppled or cried out in pain. I was with Pa in one of the storehouses that formed part of the outer wall. I had my rifle primed and cocked, but I didn't fire. There just wasn't enough hate inside my ten-year-old heart. Pa frowned and took my rifle. He fired both his gun and mine, leaving me free to reload each.

"A fine idea," Mr. Moore declared. "Josh, you do it just like Francis there. We grown men are better fit for this work."

Josh glared at me. I figured he understood why I wasn't shooting. Still, most of the men agreed it was best that a few men shoot while others reloaded. The Cherokees fell back quickly, and the whole business lasted hardly half an hour.

"It's all right," Pa told me afterward. "I can see it would be hard, shooting at shadows that might be cousins. You've got to make up your mind who you are one of these days, though, Francis. You can't be a Wataugan and a Cherokee both. Just won't do."

I told myself that if the raiders had broken through the walls and attacked Ma and Kate and my brothers, I could have fired. I wasn't entirely sure, though. I'd never really gotten the thought of that deer out of my head, and killing a fellow human being seemed a terribly hard thing to do.

Fortunately, Old Abram called off his war after two weeks and headed back home. On July 20, about the time we learned the Continental Congress had declared us an independent nation, Dragging Canoe attacked the Holston settlement at Island Flats. The settlers held their own and more. Dragging Canoe fell wounded, and it was all he could manage to escape home alive.

That August the various militias mustered.

"We're going to carry the war to the enemy," Pa explained. "You won't find many Cherokees who will follow

Dragging Canoe after we're finished."

Josh Moore shouldered his musket and followed his pa. I knew Pa hoped I would do the same. I stayed behind.

"Probably best," he said, staring out toward the hill where Charlie rested. "You can help harvest the corn. Kate and your brothers will welcome the help."

As some of the other boys going with their fathers passed our property, they taunted me.

"Cherokee Frank," they called.

I suspected Pa was right, that I would have to decide who I was one day. I was grateful, though, that the day hadn't come yet.

3

*P*A NEVER SPOKE OF that march into Cherokee country, but Josh Moore told me that the militia killed and burned like madmen. Not a village or a cornfield survived the torch, and many people who had never spoken an angry word toward us felt the sting of a rifle ball. We had no word from our cousins, and I never saw Tsula again. I could only hope that he had gone deep into Georgia and escaped the vengeful columns of angry white men.

In 1777 another treaty was signed with the Cherokees, this time at Island Flats. It seemed possible that the fighting was finally at an end. But Dragging Canoe remained alive, and there were more bitter Cherokees than ever after a starving winter.

By March 1780, when I turned fourteen, I had grown tall. Ma complained at the work she had, keeping my trousers long enough for my growing legs. There was little point to buying me boots. My feet seemed to grow daily, and I relied on moccasins that required only a little restitching to allow space for my growing toes. I was halfway between five and six feet tall when Grandma Livingstone's letter arrived.

Mail didn't come often, so any letter was an event at our farm. A letter from Grandma that arrived without birthday greetings or supplies was much more than unusual. I didn't have to read it to know something was wrong. The concern in Pa's eyes and the nervous tapping of his left boot told me so.

"Things aren't going so well for your grandmother," Ma finally announced. "There's been trouble along the coast, especially across the border in Georgia, and her help's left. All she's got left is your cousin George."

"He's no older than Francis, either," Pa remarked. I knew he was thinking that was no help at all.

"She's asked Kate to come down and give her a hand," Ma explained. "Considering all she's done for us over the years, sending cloth and trade goods and selling our hides, I can't see that we can refuse her."

I looked at Kate uneasily. Aside from a few neighbor boys, she was about the only friend I had. Not that we didn't have our fights. But Kate was the person I could tell my troubles and not fear the reply.

"I should ready my things," Kate said, staring out the window toward the mountains. "When do I leave?"

"Joe O'Hara's due to head east on Monday," Ma answered. "He knows the trails, and he's suitable company."

"He's only sixteen," Pa grumbled. "It's not proper he and Kate should travel alone."

"Nobody else's likely to go, not with planting season coming," Ma pointed out. "You can't mean to go yourself, John."

"We can spare Francis," Pa declared.

"We can?" Ma asked. "What if there's more trouble with the tribes? If you march off with the militia—"

"He wouldn't offer you much protection," Pa argued. "He's apt to like it better in Camden. He'll have plenty of new things to draw there."

I felt his words burn right through me. My little brothers looked up in surprise.

"Grandma will find work for him," Kate said, squeezing my left arm. "Francis is good at cutting wood, and he can do a bit of hunting and fishing. People at a tavern tire of corn bread and bacon."

"It's settled then," Pa announced. "They're both going."

He pocketed Grandma's letter, and Ma went to tend her kettle. Alek and Jamie resumed their lessons. I just stood there, frozen.

That night I was sitting on the porch, staring at the stars, when Kate found me.

"Consider it an adventure," she urged. "Francis, we might even get to visit Charleston. What a fine place that is supposed to be! Even Camden's a real town, not just a scattered lot of buildings. Pa's right to say you'll have new things to see and draw, too."

"He didn't mean it that way," I told her. "It's not why I'm going, either. He knows Joe O'Hara doesn't need my help, and you sure don't need protecting. Joe would sooner pick up a rattlesnake than tangle with you. No, he doesn't think I'll ever prove to be a proper mountain boy, not the way Charlie would have been. So he's sending me off for Grandma to worry over."

"Well, whatever the reason, I'll be glad of your company, little brother."

Kate drew an invisible line from the top of her head to my forehead, showing I'd spurted up right past her. Then she laughed.

"I'm not so little a brother as before," I admitted.

"Be tall as Pa when we get back."

"If we ever do come back," I said, sighing. "What if he leaves us there for good, Kate? He's got Alek and Jamie, after all."

"Much as he misses Charlie, I don't think he'd allow us to stay in Camden long."

I wasn't Charlie, though. Even if he asked Kate to return, he might well leave me to Grandma's care.

Those next three days before departing, I tried to find some way to tell Pa I didn't want to go. But each time I nerved myself enough to speak, his eyes would hush me. Ma finished making me a new shirt, and she smoked bacon for the journey.

I'll miss you two," she told me when Monday dawned. "But your grandmother needs you." I wasn't sure whom she was trying to convince.

I gave her a hug and went out to ready the horses. We would take three. Kate and I would each ride one. The third would carry hides Pa wanted to swap for goods he needed in Camden. Joe O'Hara brought along three mules carrying trade goods. Nobody left the mountains on any journey without taking things to trade. Travel was too hard not to earn a profit of some kind.

I kissed Ma good-bye and gave each of my little brothers a parting nod. Kate kissed and hugged them all. I envied her the ease with which she expressed her feelings.

"Best say something to Pa," she urged as I started to mount.

"What?" I asked.

"Something," she repeated. "Anything."

I walked over and offered my hand. He shook it, but neither of us spoke a word.

"We'll miss you," Ma called when we returned to the horses.

"Mind your grandma," Pa added. I paused a moment, hoping he might say more. He didn't, though, and when Joe led his mules eastward, I urged our packhorse after him. Kate brought up the rear.

We were a rather pitiful bunch. Even though Joe was two years older than I was, he was hardly a hair taller. Joe had red hair and a thousand freckles. His ears stuck out, too, giving him a comical appearance. Some boys would have grown mean from all the jests sent his way, but Joe just laughed.

"I may be a foolish-looking fellow, but I can read, write, and puzzle my numbers," he told me once. "Not many boys who've buried as many fathers as I have can say half as much."

It was Joe's misfortune to be born six weeks after his first father drowned fording a river. Another father caught the smallpox and died when Joe was three. The third died fighting the Shawnees. His ma had taken a new husband only last winter, although people figured his days might already be numbered.

"I've got four brothers," Joe told me once. "Only Jim and me had the same pa."

"Maybe having a lot of fathers gives you a better chance of finding one who understands you," I told Kate.

"Don't say such a thing to Joe," she warned me. "I've watched him mourn each time, and I don't find anything about being orphaned to recommend to anyone. As for Pa, well, he's hard on everyone. And he's not half as bad as you like to think."

"Half as bad is plenty," I grumbled.

Joe had been just twelve the first time he'd crossed the mountains and visited the South Carolina settlements. He'd gone alone twice since turning fifteen, so I felt that Kate and I were plenty safe in his company. Besides, I'd brought along my Dickert rifle. Joe had one of his own. They were mainly for hunting food, but nobody was ever too sure what he would find in the high country.

I had never been as far east as Roan Mountain, the tall peak you could see from the Watauga valley, and I was a little nervous about the trip. I'd heard from newcomers that people in the east called us "hill people" and laughed at our clothes and habits.

"What of it?" Kate had asked when I shared my worries.

"We'll probably laugh at them, too."

I doubted it. You might make fun of some Charleston dandy passing through the Watauga country, but you weren't apt to laugh at folks in their own valley. To make matters worse, I'd heard of card cheats and thieves who preyed on travelers.

To drive away my worries and help pass the time, I took out my mouth organ and blew a cheerful tune. Joe made up a song to go along with the melody. Although we never quite got the two to match, it did quicken our pace some. Afterward, Kate sang a ballad for us in her high, sweet voice. The music floated all around us and drifted off down the valley. Before long we began climbing, and the singing had to wait. We couldn't spare the extra breath. At best, the road was little more than a rutted trail. In March, it was mostly overgrown with spring grasses and saplings. The going was never easy, and more than once we had to lead the horses along a narrow path Joe cut through the woods with his hatchet.

We managed twenty miles or so that first day. We were still on the western slope of Roan Mountain. We camped in a meadow, and Joe shot a pair of rabbits for our supper. Kate cooked them in a stew with some potatoes and wild onions. I spent my time tending the horses and chopping wood for the cook fire. By the time night fell, we were fed and halfway warm.

"It'll be better tomorrow," Joe assured us. "We won't be this high forever. The peaks have a chill to them."

That was an understatement. I would gladly have built

up the fire so we would have had its warmth. Joe worried sparks might spread, though.

"Best we not let everybody know we're here, too," he added.

Once we crossed Roan Mountain and started our way down the eastern slope, I noticed that Joe rode ahead every few miles to scout the trail. Twice, he led us off on detours to avoid other riders.

"I don't recognize those fellows," he told us. "I never entirely trust people I don't know."

There was good reason. Our fifth day out, not far from Bald Mountain, we came across a skinny young fellow lying dead beside the trail. He had a bullet hole in his chest. There were a lot of horse tracks nearby.

"Shouldn't we stop and cover him up?" I asked Joe.

"If you do that, the ones who've done it will know someone's been by," he said. "That poor soul's past worry now. We're not."

Once we were out of the mountains and into the settled country, we learned there was more trouble waiting for us. I'd heard stories about Continental troops fighting British soldiers, but before, none of it had any real meaning. It was different as we journeyed east. The previous December, a British army had landed in Georgia and taken control of Savannah. Gen. Benjamin Lincoln had marched out from Charleston to try to retake the town. Our French allies had come to help, too. But even together, they had been unable to do any good. Afterward, parties of Tories began warring with neighboring bands of patriots throughout the South.

"Best thing to do's keep quiet and avoid everyone," Joe warned. "Most people can tell we're mountain folk by the way we talk. And Tories know we're not on their side. We've got hides and horses they'd be happy to take from us."

"Even counting Kate, we're just three," I said, glancing anxiously at the surrounding woods. "If grown men come along, what kind of fight can we make?"

"Well, if we're careful, we'll avoid company," Joe said, reining in his horse. "If we can't avoid a fight, we'll give our best. Two rifles means two shots at least. Maybe nobody wants what we've got enough to be killed for it."

I grew pale at the thought. Here Pa had sent me to Camden because he didn't figure I was up to a fight, and I was riding right into one!

I slept uneasily that night. Twice I cried out in my sleep. Finally Kate brought her blankets over beside me and held me like Ma might have done.

"You're pretty big to be acting this way," she scolded.

"I know," I confessed. "Can't much help it, Kate."

"You take Joe's tales too much to heart."

"Joe didn't make up that dead man back there," I argued. "We're still a long way from Camden, too."

"Well, we'll get there. I have feelings about these sorts of things."

"When did your feelings ever tell you what was going to happen?"

"Lots of times. Now hush and try to get some rest. We've got a lot of miles to travel tomorrow."

I knew she was at least right about that, so I closed my eyes and tried to sleep. An owl fluttered through a nearby tree, though, and I jumped to my feet.

"If you're going to act a fool, stay up and keep watch," Joe grumbled. "When you get sleepy, rouse me. I'll take a turn. Then Kate can watch awhile."

"Watch for what?" I asked.

"Hoot owls and crazed mountain boys," Joe said, laughing. "No other body's foolish enough to go running around in the dark!"

We reached Quaker Meadows that next morning, and for the first time we found something resembling a real community. Col. Charles McDowell, a well-known patriot, had his home there. A neighboring family, the Grants, invited us to pass the day with them.

"It'll give your animals a rest, and I can fatten you children a bit," Mrs. Grant told us. "Pa's just slaughtered a fat hog, and we've got plenty to eat. Well?"

Joe answered for all of us. "Be a pleasure," he said.

We passed a fine evening with the Grants, eating our fill and sleeping under cover. Kate even shared a bed with Patience Grant, who was close to her age. Joe and I were grateful for the barn because that night a fearful storm blew up. Rain and hail lashed the countryside. Even so, I slept like a dead man. Joe had a hard time shaking me to life the next morning.

"How far are you heading?" Mr. Grant asked as I began packing the horses.

"Camden," I explained. "We're going to my grandma's place."

"Be watchful, children," Mr. Grant warned. "You'll

come across more Tories as you go south. They won't care if you're five or fifty, either. You won't find mercy at their hands."

"Maybe we should head back," Kate suggested.

"We're a week gone already," Joe argued. "The country ahead is easier to travel. And we have friends there, too."

"We have to go on," I told Kate. "You know we do."

She studied my eyes a moment and then agreed. She knew as well as I did that you did as Pa said.

From the time we left Quaker Meadows, we never had a whole day without spotting a farm or riders. Mostly we kept to ourselves. Occasionally families would invite us to spend the night with them. Joe generally agreed if it was near nightfall, but he kept his rifle handy. I did the same. In spite of our fears, though, we had no trouble until we were just fifty miles from Camden. We then had a real fright!

Thunder rumbled overhead. I tied the horses and mules to trees near a small spring so they could graze and drink to their hearts' content. Joe and I placed our blankets on the side of a nearby hill. Kate slept under a rock overhang just above us.

When the rain began, we joined Kate. There wasn't room for the three of us to lie down there, so we huddled together. We avoided the worst of the rain. None of us got much sleep, though. When the rain finally relented, we fell into a deep slumber.

The cold steel of my rifle barrel roused me at dawn. An old man with a full white beard and suspicious eyes stood over us. He was holding my rifle. Joe's gun rested at his side.

"Joe?" I whispered, turning to stare into the angry eyes of my friend. Kate's eyes betrayed fear. I wasn't quite sure what to make of things.

"Got some fine hides with you," the old man said. "Come to trade?"

"Joe?" I asked again. When he didn't speak, I did. "I don't suppose it would do us much good to lie about it," I said. "We don't mean any harm to anybody, though."

"Oh?" he asked. "I suppose you'll tell me you're not bound to join up with the militia and fight King George? I suppose you're going to claim these rifles are for shooting rabbits and squirrels?"

"I didn't plan to tell anybody anything," I said, swallowing hard. My legs were wobbling, and I fought to keep my teeth from chattering. "I was taught to tend my own business."

"Well, the time for that's past," the stranger told us. "You're either for the king or not. Well?"

I stiffened my spine and tried to act bravely. I didn't manage it very well. I glanced at Kate's pleading eyes and tried to steal some of Joe's defiance.

"Well?" the old man asked again.

"I guess you might as well know," I replied. "We've no use for King George. I'm not here to kill his soldiers or fight a war, but I won't pretend to be someone I'm not. You should know, though, that's my rifle there. When it's wet, it rarely fires. So unless you have a pistol ready and primed, you'll probably not fare too well in a fight."

"Suppose not," the old man said, laughing as he returned my Dickert. "I have little need to fight any patriot, though, man or boy. I'm called Josiah Fairweather. Not the best name, considering the rain we had last night, but you should consider me a friend. Yonder five miles or so there's about fifteen horsemen you wouldn't number as such."

"I don't understand," Joe said, accepting his rifle from Mr. Fairweather.

"I'm a man few people notice," Mr. Fairweather explained. "I'm old and frail. I carry no long rifle to cause trouble with. I rarely ride. People see me and hurry past. But I see everything, my friends. And I pass the word along to those who need to know."

"You're a spy," Kate declared.

"Harsh word for it," the old man said, grinning. "Just call me eyes and ears. Eyes and ears. You've likely seen a thing or two yourselves. Anything to share?"

"Nothing that would help," Joe answered. "A few men on horseback. A farm or two. Truth is, we've stayed clear of most everyone."

"It's good to be cautious, youngsters. Your names? Just so I can pass them along," he added when he read Kate's concern.

"Joe O'Hara," Joe said. "These are my friends Kate and Francis Livingstone."

"I know a Livingstone down Camden way," Mr. Fairweather said, scratching his whiskers. "Has kin with the Carolina militia."

"Likely my uncle and cousins," Kate explained.

35

"Now, that's the sort of thing best kept to yourself," our friend the spy warned. "The way the war's fought down here, few people wear uniforms or carry colors. And when a fight's over, it's as well your enemy doesn't know it was you that was fighting. I'd advise a detour south three or four miles and then on east to the river. Be wary. Tell that relation of yours at Camden that the old hawk is still about."

"You know Grandma well?" I asked.

"More years than you've been alive," he said, grinning even wider. "Maybe we'll meet again when there's time to get properly acquainted. Now, along with you, children. And watch out for Tories!"

We vowed to do just that. We crossed the last fifty miles to Camden in three days. We never passed a night with anyone after meeting Mr. Fairweather, and we avoided the main roads and well-marked trails. Most of those miles, I was totally lost. But Joe never failed to sense where he was. We appeared at Camden the very afternoon he told us we would.

Camden was a market town with a few small houses and some county buildings. Col. Joseph Kershaw, the town's principal citizen, had a tall house of considerable dimensions. Otherwise, Grandma Livingstone's tavern was as big a building as any other.

English taverns had the habit of hanging large painted signs over their doors to indicate their names, and Grandma's sign showed a deer's head. WHITE STAG, it read.

"We're here," Kate declared.

Grandma's Tavern

"Finally," I said.

"Go on and greet your grandma," Joe told us. "I'll tend to the horses."

"I should help," I told him.

"Go on," he said, pointing to the door.

Kate was already racing toward the porch. I rolled out of the saddle and turned toward the front door as it cracked open. A thin blond boy about my age peered out and yelled, "It's them!"

"At last!" a woman's voice shouted. Feet pounded on floorboards, and a smallish white-haired woman of near sixty bounded out the door. Before I quite knew what was happening, Grandma Livingstone was wrapping her arms around Kate and motioning Joe and me to her side.

"Lord, children, three of you? You've brought company, Kate?"

"My brother Francis," Kate said, waving me toward Grandma.

"The one who likes to draw," she said, smiling widely. "What a wonderful surprise. And this other one?"

"Joe O'Hara," Joe said, touching the brim of his hat. "You remember. I visited you with my stepfather, Luke Nolan."

"Indeed," Grandma said. "You won't be staying, though, I suspect."

"Got trading to do, and goods to get home," Joe said. "Just the same, I'd be grateful for a bed tonight."

"We have those," Grandma said, making room under one arm for me to burrow. "I'm so glad you've arrived. I've been worried."

"It was a long way," Kate explained.

"And no doubt full of adventures," Grandma added.

4

E SPENT THE REST OF that first day
telling Grandma about our long journey over the mountains to Camden.
From time to time, she grinned. She
broke into a broad smile when we shared the story of Mr.
Fairweather, the spy.

"I'm surprised someone hasn't hung that old crow," she
said.

We also met George McKinney, our cousin. He was
the boy who had opened the door. George was Pa's sister
Anne's youngest boy. His father, my uncle Hugh, farmed
up in North Carolina. Uncle Hugh gave me my middle
name.

"I've been living with Grandma two years now," George
explained that night when he led me upstairs to an empty
room we would share. "To tell the truth, I was glad to be
sent to Camden. Work here's no easier, but you meet a lot
of interesting people. Back on the farm, I spent most of my
time watching corn grow and running from my big brothers."

39

George

George didn't expect to remain at the tavern much longer, though.

"Pa wrote me that he and my brothers John and Will have signed on with General Caswell's militia. They're rumored to be on their way here. When they come, I'll sign up, too."

"I don't think I'd make a very good soldier, George," I confessed. "I can see why a man has to shoot a deer or a rabbit to feed his family, but shooting a man? I'd have to be awful mad at anybody to do that."

"Wouldn't you fight to protect your family?" George asked. "If the British march up here, would you just stand by and watch them? What about Grandma? Kate?"

I hung my head. I couldn't tell him about Old Abram's Cherokee raiders. I didn't want to sound like a coward.

"Well?" he asked.

"I don't know, George."

He sat down on the corner of the bed and stared hard at me. Finally, he waved me over and turned down the bedding.

"You'll change your mind," he told me, "once you learn what the Tories have done."

I heard quite a bit about the Tories that spring.

Camden was a patriot stronghold, and Grandma's neighbors had little use for Tories or King George. The town boasted a large powder magazine, a kind of underground storehouse where arms and gunpowder were kept for the use of the state militia. A few militiamen were always on guard there, and about a dozen others hung around town most days. Riders from Charleston came every few days with news. Unfortunately, most of it was bad.

As if the loss of Savannah and most of Georgia to the British wasn't bad enough, almost nine thousand British and Tory troops had landed on the South Carolina coast. Some marched down to reinforce the armies in Georgia, but most headed for Charleston. General Lincoln had sent for help, and the regular army troops from the Carolinas and Virginia had come south to aid in Charleston's defense. The trouble was that Lincoln got himself trapped inside the city. The defenses had been neglected to the point that Colonel Moultrie's fort on Sullivans Island surrendered without firing a shot. The British fleet sailed inside the harbor, and their army cut off retreat from the land side. The British fired cannons into the city and captured one of our forts after another.

"General Lincoln won't hold out much longer," a youngish lieutenant explained between sips of ale. "Already you see militia scampering westward. Once Charleston surrenders, there won't be any stopping the British. They'll march through the Carolinas just like they've done in Georgia. What's more, there are plenty of folks who will welcome them. A few weeks ago, this tavern was full of patriotic men vowing to fight the British to the death. Where are they now? Hiding in cellars or headed for the mountains!"

Afterward, when the last of the customers had left, Grandma called us together.

"I'm sorry to have put you children in such peril," she said. "I never imagined things could grow so dark as this."

"Maybe we should all leave," Kate suggested. "It's a hard journey westward into the mountains, but Francis and I know the way. We could manage it."

"Well, I'm not going anywhere," George declared. "General Caswell's coming. He'll be along soon and lift the siege. If Lincoln can hold on a little longer, we may yet win."

"There's faint hope of that," Grandma said. "Still, how can I abandon my home and property? Once, when the English drove us out of the Highlands, I gave up everything. I won't do it again."

"Seems to me," Kate said, "you escaped with your life. You can always build a new tavern. It would be nice to have you closer, Grandma. If all this trouble is coming, we should leave it behind us."

"Dear, I'm not the sort to flee. It may be a bitter tonic, seeing the Tories and the redcoats marching about like they own this country again, but in time we'll drive them out."

Although she said the words forcefully, I could tell she didn't really believe them. Still, Kate wouldn't leave Grandma behind. I certainly wasn't leaving on my own. So we remained at Grandma's tavern to await whatever fate lay ahead.

That week, we were busy every moment. If we weren't serving the militia or patriot families headed west, then George and I would be splitting logs, chopping vegetables, or fishing. It was hard to imagine how Grandma and George had managed on their own.

"A month ago all four upstairs rooms were full of guests," George told me. "At dinner, every chair was filled with a paying customer. There was barely time to get everything done. Between cooking and serving and cleaning up, I thought I would collapse!"

Only one of the upstairs rooms had a guest during the past two weeks. And no one stayed more than a single night.

"Better for us," George declared. "I don't favor sleeping on the porch or in the barn on these wet, cold nights."

"They're nothing to what we experienced in the mountains," I said, shivering at the recollection.

"Suppose not," George said. "Still, I never complain about sleeping on a feather mattress. Even if I have to share it with you!"

"At least I don't snore," I said, laughing.

I had hoped to do some drawing once we reached Camden, but there was rarely time. I'd start off chopping wood or helping George with some job like mending battered shutters. It was kind of comical, watching him barking instructions at me. Although he was actually a month older than I was, George was a full four inches shorter. He had a reddish tint to his blond hair and a thousand freckles.

"There's nothing comical about them," he complained when we fished in the river south of town. "Every

Livingstone I ever knew except you had them! Are you sure we're related?"

"Probably not," I told him. "At least that's what my pa would say. I have my Cherokee grandma's hair and eyes. And I don't make a very good farmer."

"Well, you've got time to learn," George assured me. "You do your share of the work. Any good with that rifle you brought with you?"

"I can hit what I aim at."

"Then we'll do some hunting. Fresh meat would be welcome. Nothing better to do."

Usually when we finished our daily chores, we took our poles to the river. George knew all the best fishing spots, and he could swim like an otter. I knew enough to keep myself from drowning, but I mostly favored dry land. When it came to shooting squirrels and rabbits, though, I put him to shame.

"Lead's hard to come by in the high country," I told George when he missed his second shot. "You dare not miss. You're apt to go hungry. Your trouble is that you don't get close enough. Once you see your quarry, circle around so the wind is in your face. That way, you don't give off scent. Then creep in close and wait for the animal to come to you. Once it's there, you take your shot."

"But how can you be sure a squirrel is going to do what you expect?" George asked.

"I guess from knowing squirrels. It's hard to put into words. You do know, though, George. My Cherokee cousin Tsula taught me. He said to say a silent prayer, too, offering thanks for the gift of that creature's life. I know

44

that you think it addled. My friends back home did, too. But I hit what I aim at."

"I don't make fun of such things," George said, nodding solemnly. "Pa told me to always mount my horse on the right side. One time I didn't, and the fool animal threw me into a nettle patch. Does no good to ask for trouble. No, sir."

One sunny afternoon the second week of May, George and I finished our chores early and set off for the river. We hardly got a mile from the tavern when we saw three horsemen galloping up the Charleston road. George pulled me into a grove of willows and whispered, "Shhh." We waited silently until the riders got close. Then George sighed and stepped out into the road, waving and whistling.

"Captain Henderson!" George called. "It's me! George McKinney."

"George? Boy, what are you doing out here alone?" the man asked. "Don't you know the whole British army's apt to be marching along here any moment?"

"What?" George cried.

"General Lincoln's called it quits, son. Surrendered the whole army. Five thousand men! And I hear the redcoats didn't lose a hundred men fighting! We've done them more damage raiding their supplies. Now they don't have Charleston to bother with, they'll be tending to us. And to our friends."

"Charleston's fallen?" I asked.

"My cousin Francis," George explained, shoving me forward. "Come to help Grandma."

"If you boys plan to stay here, you'd best hide those

rifles," the captain warned. "It won't take long for the Tories to get their courage up. They'll grab every man, woman, or child with a rifle and take them to the prison hulks. And those known to sympathize with our cause are sure to meet with a bad end."

As the men rode off, George explained, "It's said that down in Georgia, the Tories hanged every patriot they could capture. They took their stock, burned their houses and barns, and killed those unwilling to swear oaths to the king."

"Kate was right," I said, sighing. "We should have gone home when we could."

"Well, you still can," George replied. "Me, I plan to find General Caswell and join Pa and my brothers. Seems to me they'll need every rifle they can raise. You can shoot, Francis. Now that you know what's at stake, you're bound to see the need."

"I'm no kind of soldier," I insisted. "And we're too young."

"Younger boys are serving, Francis. And you can shoot as good as a man. Seems to me it's your duty."

"Only duty I've got is to protect my sister and Grandma."

"Well, I guess you've got a right to be scared."

"I'm not scared!" I said.

"Well, you couldn't prove it to me. Anyway, we best go back and tell Grandma the news. I've lost all interest in fishing."

"Sure," I agreed. And so we returned to the tavern.

We had no need to relay the news. Captain Henderson

and his companions were making their way around Camden, sharing the word of General Lincoln's surrender. Being a patriot stronghold and one of the few towns of any substance in central South Carolina, Camden was certain to be an early target of the British and their Tory allies.

"What are we going to do, Grandma?" I asked.

"Well, first you take those rifles down to the root cellar and put them safely away. There's a trapdoor under the flour barrels. George knows where. You hide any powder, lead, knives, or anything else a redcoat could consider a weapon. I'll send Kate along with my silver. Pewter is good enough for any English guests."

"Yes, ma'am," I said, frowning.

"George, when you finish, I want you to take those two good horses we have stabled at Colonel Kershaw's barn and hide them out in the swamps. Hobble them so they can't run far. We may need them. I don't expect to be troubled. After all, if the English come, they won't want to do their own cooking and such. But it's a foolish Scotsman who doesn't have a fast horse nearby. Eh, George?"

"Yes, Grandma," George agreed.

"Francis, you ready your horses. Kate's, too. Follow George and hobble the animals where he shows you."

"Yes, ma'am," I answered.

Afterward, we hid the rifles, several hunting and skinning knives, and even a heavy sword Grandma had placed over the fireplace downstairs. Kate brought all the silver and some china plates. We greased up our rifle barrels to hold off the rust. We wrapped the knives in blankets. George placed the sword, which had belonged to our

grandpa Livingstone, in a bearskin. We dug a hole for the
chest holding the china and silver. It would be a time
before we needed those. But the weapons might come in
handy at any minute.

During the three days that followed, we witnessed a
terrible exodus westward. Whole families walked with
their meager belongings, hoping to find refuge with relatives or compassionate farmers. George and I fetched our
rifles and hunted every morning. Then we returned the
guns to the cellar. Kate helped Grandma cook venison and
rabbits. We ate very little of the food. Grandma gave all
she could spare to the fleeing women and children.

A few parties of horsemen rode by, too, most of them
claiming to be headed for some distant reorganization of
the army. Their eyes betrayed their fear, though, and when
George questioned them about General Caswell's North
Carolina militia, they had no answer. The Camden garrison also left, taking what powder they could with them.

"Running away," George observed. "If they'd get themselves organized, we could still give the British a fight of it."

If anger won battles, George could have beaten the
whole British army by himself. It didn't, though. And we
soon saw proof of just how badly the British had whipped
the patriots at Charleston.

I was out splitting logs for Grandma's cook fires when
I spied a column of dust rising from the Charleston road. I
thought that it might be another cavalry detachment fleeing west. I set aside my ax and turned toward the tavern.

"Best we stay here," George said, frowning. "That's a lot

of horses coming. In a hurry, too. I don't expect them to be friendly to our cause this time."

"British?" I asked.

"Or Tories," George said, spitting a sour taste from his mouth. "Either way, we ought to be the first to meet them. Grandma and Kate should stay inside."

I'm not sure how George knew these riders wouldn't be friendly, but he did. There were close to thirty of them, and their leader wore a tattered green uniform coat.

"Well, we've arrived in time after all," the man in the green coat declared. "I expected Camden to be empty. Word is that it's as fine a nest of traitors as exists in all the Carolinas."

The man spoke like most Carolinians. That sent shudders down my spine. If not for his green coat, he looked just like one of Captain Henderson's men. If you couldn't tell one side from the other unless they wore a uniform, how could you spot the enemy?

"Can we help you, sir?" George asked.

"Ah, the traitor speaks," the Tory leader responded. "You can announce our arrival. I'm Captain Jarvis of His Majesty's American Legion. My men and I will need some refreshment."

"We've got a good well there," George explained, pointing it out. "Cool, fresh water."

"Fill a trough for the horses then," Captain Jarvis barked. "As for us, we will want something a bit more refined."

The riders laughed.

"You'll keep in mind that South Carolina is no longer a

colony of rebels," Jarvis added, studying me with threatening eyes. "Things will be different here now."

"Your horse, sir?" I said, reaching out for the reins. My movement spooked his mount, and the animal reared up, spilling its rider into a pile of kindling. As for the horse itself, it bolted off down the road.

"After it," Jarvis shouted, and two riders started in pursuit. The others tried to keep from laughing as the fuming officer fought to regain his feet. He fell twice. Finally, a couple of his men helped him escape the woodpile. They entered the tavern while George and I, together with three of the Tory cavalry, attended to the horses. We poured two buckets of well water into a wooden trough and left the animals to drink.

Two of the Tories were about seventeen and paid little attention to us. The third was a younger fellow around my age. He was closer to George's size, and he looked us over the way a hungry cat might eye a mouse. The others were dressed in simple homespun wool breeches and coats, but our young guest wore stiff cotton pants and a tailored cloth coat.

"You two are rebels?" he finally asked.

"Rebels?" I asked. "Rebels against what?"

"Not what," the young Tory replied. "Whom. King George, of course."

The boy had a polished accent and spoke like someone much older. There was something about his penetrating gaze that made me nervous.

"I never had much time to consider such things," I said,

avoiding his eyes. "My grandma keeps me too busy."

"And when she doesn't," George added, "thirty thirsty soldiers arrive."

"It's as well for you that you haven't taken up arms," our young visitor told us. "We've killed four men since leaving Charleston. Yesterday we hanged a boy who was spying on us. It's difficult to tell friend from foe. One of the men recognized him, though. His family are all rebels."

"You hanged him?" I asked. "How old was he?"

"Perhaps as old as you," the Tory replied. "Something to consider, eh?"

"Yes," George agreed.

"Traitors have had a fine time of it these past five years," the Tory went on to say. "Now we'll show them what price must be paid for such disloyalty."

He picked up a splinter of wood and broke it in half. His companions laughed.

I could see George redden. I hoped he wouldn't say something that would get us into trouble. I could tell he was fuming inside. But the Tories had rifles, and we had only our tongues. It was a poor match.

The Tory horsemen stayed three hours. They ate and drank what they wanted, and they paid for none of it. As they left, Grandma presented the captain a bill.

"Loyal citizens never ask money from their soldiers," Captain Jarvis said, tearing the paper into pieces. "You would do well, madam, to remember who's in command here now!"

The officer then tried to mount his horse. His foot

missed the stirrup, though, and he fell flat on his face. This time the men laughed heartily.

"Silence!" the captain shouted. "Find me a proper horse, Lieutenant Ross!"

To my surprise, the boyish Tory galloped off toward the Kershaw place, followed by five other men. They returned with three fine animals, and the Tory captain chose a fast gray mare particularly favored by Colonel Kershaw.

"Move my saddle to the gray!" Jarvis told George. He reluctantly did as instructed. Afterward, when the Tories departed, George stared at them hatefully.

"Probably best I didn't have my rifle," he said, kicking a rock down the road. "I would surely have killed that fool."

"And the rest of them would have killed you, George," I pointed out.

"I know that," he admitted. "That's why I'm glad I didn't have the rifle."

"You probably would have missed, too."

"Could be," he agreed. "Either way, it would have brought you harm. They would have burned the tavern, too. And as for Kate and Grandma—"

"You did well, holding your temper, George," I said, nodding. "It would have been a bad swap."

"He's in command," George pointed out.

"Him?" I asked, laughing. "He can't even command his own horse. I don't know who's made him a captain, but I hope there are more such fellows in charge. We stand a fair chance against that sort. It was that young fellow who gave me a chill. Hanged a boy our age, he said, with not even a hint of sympathy. Those are the ones who scare me."

"Me, too," George agreed.

On June 1, we had our first look at the regular British army. Gen. Charles Cornwallis, who had been left in command of the army stationed in the South, arrived at the head of thousands of smartly dressed soldiers. There were regiments from England, Scotland, and even a group of Irish volunteers. There were also Tories, some of them outfitted in green coats and white trousers. Others looked like mounted farmers carrying their bird guns. There were more of them than I could count, though, and it was hard not to feel trapped.

Cornwallis moved into Colonel Kershaw's fine two-story house a quarter mile from the tavern. British soldiers confiscated most of the other buildings in town. Tories rode around, burning and robbing every patriot farm in sight. Poor Colonel Kershaw was sent away as a prisoner. We weren't ignored, either. Tory officers took over the upstairs rooms for their use. Kate and Grandma slept in the narrow storeroom. George and I stretched a square of canvas over poles behind the cookhouse and slept on the bare ground. Considering the heat, I only halfway minded.

Although the British marched off in various directions, establishing forts and outposts to control the whole colony, a considerable force remained at Camden. As for the others, they busied themselves terrorizing our friends. Col. Banastre Tarleton and a band of loyalist cavalry caught a column of patriot reinforcements headed for

Charleston in the Waxhaws country and slaughtered them. I listened with horror when Tarleton's cavalrymen boasted of how they had cut down a hundred men or more with their sabers. Those who tried to surrender were killed anyway. After that, people called the colonel "Bloody Ban" and spoke of "Tarleton's quarter," meaning the Tories took no prisoners.

I'll never forget the first time Colonel Tarleton came to the tavern. He arrived with two other officers. Immediately most of the customers, Tories who had lately relocated to Camden, abandoned their tables and stepped outside to finish their tankards of ale on the porch. I suppose they knew what was coming. Another dozen of Tarleton's green-uniformed soldiers soon arrived.

Tarleton himself wasn't a man who stood out in a crowd. Short, rather stocky, and not yet thirty years old, he didn't seem like the kind of man to spread terror throughout South Carolina. But when I walked over to remove two abandoned tankards from the table he selected, he gazed at me with a hard look.

"Send the girl," he said, pointing to Kate. "A boy like you shouldn't be serving soldiers in a tavern. You should be out in the field with all other loyal subjects of the king, putting an end to this rebellion."

I nodded politely and reached for the tankards. He grabbed my hand in an iron grip and squeezed until I cried out.

"Do as I say, boy," he barked. "And do it now!"

I hurried over to Kate.

"He's a mean one," I warned.

"So I've heard," she answered.

Kate strode to the table with her tray and carried away the tankards. When the colonel started to speak, she ignored him and returned to the bar.

"Not wise," George whispered.

Colonel Tarleton rose from his chair, made a mock bow in our direction, and kicked a chair across the floor.

"Perhaps it's not possible for a king's officer to receive civil treatment here," he declared. "Well, my boys, shall we show these insulting children what's expected of them?"

The men laughed, but Grandma marched out with a bottle of wine and offered it to the colonel.

"Pardon them, sir," she said, smiling politely. "My grandchildren are from the mountains. They aren't accustomed to serving. I wouldn't have them here, except you know how difficult it is to get reliable help. And I've heard the mountains are full of outlaws and traitors now."

"Indeed," the colonel said, accepting the wine. "But we'll soon deal with them. Send the girl back, won't you, so that I can instruct her in what's required."

Grandma lost her smile. With the tavern full of Tarleton's soldiers, there really wasn't anything else to do. Kate returned, and the colonel had her sit and talk. Later I asked what he wanted, and she just glared.

"No need you knowing," she told me. "I wouldn't do it. He may be a colonel and a fine man for ordering soldiers and hurting boys, but he's no one I would want to walk with. He's got plenty of women, as I hear it. He'll have to do without me."

The truth was, though, that we all dreaded the day the

British or Tory soldiers pushed us to the point of resisting. George was never far from exploding, and I knew that I wouldn't stand for anyone mistreating Grandma or Kate.

"If one of them lays a hand on you, I'll make him regret it," I told Kate.

"You'd accomplish nothing by that," she scolded. "Just get yourself hanged. Haven't you heard about that Henley boy upriver? Tories broke into his house, and he tried to stop them from taking his mother's silver. They dragged him outside and hanged him from an oak tree. He was twelve! There's no use in fighting them, Francis. Not here and now. But I've heard General Washington's sent us help. Maybe then we'll teach these invaders some manners."

Rumors of a new patriot army heading south from Virginia came and went. We saw neither hide nor hair of any Continental army. Not even a militia company appeared. Colonel Marion, whose first name was also Francis, led some horsemen against British supply wagons and outposts. Col. Thomas Sumter was closer still. But even joined together, they were no match for the garrison at Camden. They certainly couldn't defeat Cornwallis's entire army.

By the end of July, we felt desperate. News continued to spread of an army led by General de Kalb hurrying down from Virginia. We then heard that Gen. Horatio Gates, the hero of Saratoga, was on his way. Some said ten thousand soldiers were marching south. But I doubted it was true. Listening to our British guests boast about slaughtering bands of patriot militia made me cringe.

One night the first week of August, I was fast asleep beside George when someone stirred me to life. I started to cry out, but a hand muffled my words. Across from me a sleepy George was coming to life. Another shadowy figure knelt on the ground beside him.

"It's all right," George whispered. "My brothers."

I shook myself awake and tried to focus my eyes on our visitors. The two of them did resemble George, but they were somewhat taller and older. John McKinney was eighteen. An inch shy of six feet tall, he reminded me an awful lot of Pa. His sixteen-year-old brother, Will, was three inches shorter and skinny as a fence rail. They were both happy to see George. They were less pleased to learn that the British had fortified Camden.

"There'll be a battle soon," John told us. "General Caswell's about to meet up with the Maryland and Delaware Continentals under General Gates. More militia's coming, too. We'll gobble up these outposts and chase old Cornwallis right back to Charleston. Then we'll see whose turn it is to surrender."

It was good to hear such spirited talk. But the purpose of my cousins' visit was to gather food.

"We're near starving," John admitted. "Half the boys are barefoot, and we're short on shot and powder, too."

"We don't have much," I replied. "But I'm sure Grandma would want you to have it all."

"We take recruits, too, Francis," Will added. "George, you're coming?"

"Soon as I crawl to the house and fetch my rifle," George replied.

"Francis?" John asked.

"I'm bound to stay," I said, avoiding their eyes.

"He's a hair young," George added. "Maybe after Grandma and Kate are safe."

"Maybe," I said, not really convinced that would make a difference.

I helped George and his brothers collect what flour and meat we had on hand. It wasn't much, and I could see they were disappointed. John and Will set off ahead to make sure the road out of town was clear. George remained long enough to say good-bye.

George stood there, provision bag over one shoulder. The coat that didn't quite fit anymore failed to reach his belt buckle. I couldn't help wishing he would change his mind and remain with us. Those past weeks we had become more like brothers than cousins.

"Don't worry about staying behind," he said as he gripped my hand. "We could use you, but I feel better knowing you're here. We'll see each other soon, too."

"Hope so," I replied as he turned to go. "Try not to get yourself shot."

He turned and grinned. Then he hurried off to join his brothers.

5

AWN FOUND ME SITTING on my blankets, feeling terribly alone. I suppose, in a way, George had been the big brother I had missed since Charlie died. We shared the heavy work at the tavern and passed most afternoons fishing or swimming or hunting mischief. Now that he was gone, I found myself with all the work and half the hands to do it.

"Now you know what it was like for George before you came," Grandma told me when I complained. "Do what you can. What you can't, we'll find a way to do without."

It wasn't just the old chores that kept me busy. Some new Tory officer appeared each day at the tavern. Often as not, he'd insist I polish his boots or tend to his horse.

"Pa once said no man worth half a cent leaves his mount to another's care," Kate said when I returned from one such errand.

"These men ride their horses hard, and they use their spurs on them, Kate. If one horse breaks down, they just

steal another from a nearby farm."

"We might have to do something about that," Kate said, laughing. "I wonder if you could find some nettle or maybe a burr or two to place under their saddle blankets."

"You'd only punish the horse," I said, frowning. "It's not *its* fault."

In truth, I didn't have the courage to challenge the Tories or the British soldiers stationed at Camden. I'd heard too many stories of beatings and hangings of rebel boys. With General Gates on his way to drive the enemy back to Charleston, I thought it a foolish thing, getting shot or hanged the week before.

Kate was more defiant. She wasn't afraid to spill a bowl of hot soup on an ill-mannered soldier. And when a lieutenant delivered his company's laundry for washing, she dropped each clean garment in a patch of poison oak. Seven men broke out in painful rashes.

"Take care, child," Grandma warned. "These enemies of ours are prideful men. If they discover what you've done, you might come to regret it."

"Hah!" Kate replied. "There's poison oak everywhere in the summer. How can they prove it's my doing?"

I noticed that they didn't bring laundry to the tavern afterward, though.

August brought on a spell of terrible heat. The Carolina Tories took it in stride, but those from northern colonies like New York and New Jersey grew feverish. It was especially hard on the English. They rarely paraded and only occasionally drilled. A handful were always down at the river, trying to cool off, and there were lines of men

waiting to fill water barrels at our well.

For a time our porch was used as a hospital, but the officers enjoyed drinking at the tavern and ordered the sick men removed. It wasn't long before the air soured with an odd smell.

"The odor of death," Grandma called it. One evening she stared at the crows collecting on the bare branch of a dead elm and frowned.

"What is it?" I asked.

"A bad omen," she said, gripping my shoulders. "I saw crows gather like that the day before your grandfather died. They know a battle's coming. Something terrible is about to happen, Francis, and there isn't a thing in the world any of us can do to prevent it."

I only half believed her. It seemed to me that if General Gates attacked the British when so many were sick, he was bound to win. But although couriers rode into Camden, announcing Gates was coming, the hero of Saratoga seemed in no great hurry to arrive. General Cornwallis, on the other hand, sprang to action. He had been in Charleston for weeks, but he and his staff rode into Camden like madmen. They arrived late the night of August 13. Rather than rest, though, the general shouted orders and sent couriers off in seemingly every direction. Soon the scattered British detachments reassembled north of town.

They left Camden two days later, determined to fight.

"You have to admit he's a brave man, the general," a sick corporal told me when I brought him a dipper of well water that night. "Gates is up there with five or six thousand men.

We've got half that many, and near eight hundred are sick. A cautious man would turn back to Charleston, but the general won't leave us to the rebels."

I knew he was thinking what some of the sick men were saying aloud. After Tarleton's slaughter of those Virginians, no captured soldier in Cornwallis's army, even the sick or wounded, could expect mercy.

Early the next morning the ground shook with the thunder of cannons. I learned later that the battle took place more than five miles north of town. It was hard to believe, for the wind carried the sounds of musket and rifle fire, punctuated by cannons. I hoped and prayed that once the noise died away, we would see Uncle Hugh and the rest of General Caswell's men chase the routed British through town. When the sounds of gunfire melted away, the first men staggering into Camden were redcoats. They didn't display a trace of panic, though. Instead, they carried wounded and dying comrades to makeshift hospitals. Even bleeding men had smiles on their faces, and when a company of green-shirted Tory cavalry arrived, they were laughing and boasting as never before. When the dust from their horses' hooves settled, I saw they had driven fifty or so weary prisoners into town. Among them was George McKinney.

"Grandma," I called, hurrying inside the tavern. "Grandma!"

"You haven't brought good news, have you?" she asked.

Kate emerged from the storeroom and read my solemn eyes.

"What's happened?" she asked.

"We've lost," I said, staring at my toes. "The redcoats are laughing, and Tories brought in prisoners. They have George."

"Where?" Grandma asked.

"Over by the Kershaw barn," I explained. "I'll go see if they'll allow me to visit him."

"No," Grandma said, grabbing my arm to hold me there. "Best to wait. It won't go well for any of us if they discover we have kin among their enemies."

I turned to Kate, hoping for encouragement. She agreed with Grandma, though. It was well past noon before I persuaded them to let me go. By then, returning officers had filled the tavern, and dozens of captives were assembled at the Kershaw place. I filled a cask with water and headed in that direction. A British sergeant stopped me and sent me instead toward a sea of wounded redcoats.

"Don't give any to the men with belly wounds," a surgeon warned me. "See the others have a drink, though. Bathe their foreheads as well."

I nodded.

It was an awful sight, those lines of wounded men. Even though they were my enemies, I couldn't feel any hatred for them. Most were no more than eighteen, and several had ghastly wounds. One poor boy moaned and clutched his fife as I offered him a drink. A rifle ball had smashed his jaw and broken all the teeth on the left side of his mouth. He managed to mutter a thank-you anyway.

I spent the rest of the day carrying water to the wounded. Only at dusk did I slip away and creep to the Kershaw barn. By then more than a hundred prisoners had been collected there. A few were Maryland Continentals. Dressed in blue uniforms, they formed their own small circle away from the militia. I tried to approach the larger group, part of General Caswell's North Carolinians, but a young British private stopped me.

"They're to receive nothing," he barked. "Rebels merit no consideration."

"Are you ordering me not to offer them water?" I asked.

"Ordering?" the private asked.

"I only ask because a colonel sent me over with this keg. I'm to offer the rebels a drink. If you're saying I shouldn't, though, I'll happily head home."

"A colonel ordered you here?" the young redcoat asked. "Which colonel?"

"Oh, how would I know?" I asked. "One officer or another has been ordering me around all day."

"Well, you had best go ahead and mind the colonel," the guard finally said. "No point in angering an officer. They do appear thirsty."

And so I made my way among the North Carolinians. Soon I located George. I passed along the keg to another and sat beside my cousin.

"George, what happened?" I asked.

"Pa's dead. Will and John, too."

"How?"

"It's hard to explain," he said. "I was there, and I don't believe it happened. We had them outnumbered. We were confident of victory. It wasn't even dawn, though, and many of the men were weak from sickness. First the Tory cavalry charged, but we beat them back. There was some shooting. But both sides then pulled back to wait for dawn. Once we could see, you could just sense the dismay. We thought we were attacking the Camden garrison, but the whole British army was waiting for us. And when they started that awful steady march, bayonets glinting in the sun, one rank after another of the militia fell back. Some dropped their guns and ran for the hills. The Continentals on the right held, but I don't think a dozen men in my company stayed. We didn't stand a chance. A redcoat bayoneted John right beside me. Another knocked my rifle away and would have killed me but for his lieutenant, who ordered me held as a prisoner.

"I don't know everything that happened, but General Gates and most of the army took off like rabbits. General de Kalb rallied his men and held off the whole British force for a time. They shot him five or six times, I hear, and then bayoneted him. Some say he's still alive, but it's hard to believe. The Maryland and Delaware Continentals did most of the killing and most of the dying. Hundreds of them are lying out there, I hear. I feel just terrible, Francis. Pa's dead. My brothers are dead. And for what? Now Cornwallis can march into North Carolina and even Virginia. There's nothing to stop him. Ma's home all alone. And there's talk we'll all be hanged!"

George leaned against me and sobbed. One of the older men tried to offer a comforting hand, but George pushed him away.

"Keg's empty," one of the North Carolina boys said, tapping its side. "Son, you best get along home now before they forget you're only a visitor."

"George, maybe you can come with me," I suggested.

"No, there's been enough running away today," he said, rubbing his eyes dry. "Tell Grandma I'm all right. Take care of her."

"I'll do what I can," I promised. Then I heaved the empty keg onto my shoulder and started back to the tavern. The guard stopped me and inspected my pockets.

"Some try to pass messages," he explained. "Captain Jarvis was none too happy to hear the prisoners received water. He recognized you, too. I hope you can recall the name of that colonel. Otherwise you're sure to have trouble over this."

I returned to the tavern with a heavy heart and a dread of what lay ahead. When I got to the porch, I found two Tories waiting.

"Captain Jarvis is waiting inside," the first said. "Come along."

As if to encourage my progress, the second Tory poked my ribs with the barrel of his musket. I stumbled inside the tavern and approached Captain Jarvis. He was sitting at the corner table with his young lieutenant.

"Ah, did you find your colonel?" the captain asked.

"There was no colonel," I answered. "I just couldn't stand seeing thirsty men. And before you start calling me a traitor, ask the surgeons. I spent most of the day giving water to the British wounded."

"That's true," a thin-faced officer from one of the other tables declared. "I saw him myself. I thought he was perhaps an officer's son come along to view the spectacle, until I saw his feet."

66

I gazed down at my moccasins and frowned.

"Well, I'm delighted to know he's eager to serve the king," Jarvis said. "We're seeking volunteers for a particularly nasty chore tomorrow, aren't we, Lieutenant Ross?"

"I thought we were using prisoners," the lieutenant answered.

"We'll use whomever I choose," Jarvis insisted. "Have one of the men watch him. I wouldn't want him slipping away during the night."

"Harvey," the lieutenant said, nodding to the Tory who had jabbed my ribs. "Tie him to one of the wagons. We'll want him early tomorrow."

George had once suggested that spending a little time around the Tories would send me rushing into the militia ranks. I learned what he had meant those next two days. As if being tied to a wagon all night wasn't punishment enough, the next morning I was marched north to the battlefield. There, together with a dozen boys from neighboring farms and a few prisoners, I was forced to dig graves for the fallen British and Tory soldiers. The young lieutenant watched us every minute, pointing out each of our errors with glee. He insisted the graves be dug three feet deep and lined up neatly in rows. We then dragged the swollen and torn remains of our enemies and deposited them in the cold ground. The heat and smell overpowered me, and I became sick.

It took us all that day and most of the following morning. Only after burying the enemy dead were we sent to collect the heaps of dead Continentals. I think the Tory lieutenant intended that the few dozen militiamen killed in the battle be left as they lay. When one of the prisoners headed in that direction, though, I followed. Together, we started digging.

"No need for separate graves," a British sergeant said, joining us. "I'd dig quickly, too, lads. That baby-faced officer will soon notice what you're up to."

"Won't you be in trouble for this, too?" I asked.

"Oh, the general can do without a Tory lieutenant easier than he can spare Sergeant O'Halloran," the redcoat said, grinning. "I won't say these fellows deserve much praise for their conduct in battle, but dead's dead. And I hate the sight of bones on a battlefield."

We dug a solitary hole. The ground was mushy, for we were near a bog, and that made the work go swiftly. We could collect only fourteen corpses before the young Tory arrived. Among them, though, were my uncle Hugh and two cousins.

I wanted to offer some prayer, say something meaningful, but I felt so empty. Their lifeless eyes haunted me. I remembered Charlie and the fence. I finally sank to my knees, crying.

"Rest a bit," one of the others suggested. I blinked my eyes dry and picked up the spade. I saw so much of George in their faces. What if the British hanged him? And what would they do to me?

"You were to stay with the others!" the lieutenant shouted. "These rebels should have been left here as a warning to others."

"Fine enough for you," the sergeant replied. "You'll be riding off into the countryside. My company's to remain here on garrison duty. Do you think we want the smell of these sort ruining our breakfast?"

"I hadn't considered that," the lieutenant noted. "When they finish, bring them back."

"I know my duty, sir," Sergeant O'Halloran answered.

And so we shoveled dirt over my uncle, cousins, and their companions. We piled stones atop the grave in the old Scottish fashion Pa had often described. The sergeant sent his prisoner off to join the others. He kept me behind.

"It's a fit marker," the sergeant declared. "We've a burial cairn or two in Ireland, you know. The Scots favor them."

"You've seen a lot of battles, I suppose," I said. "What makes a man want to be a soldier?"

"Ah, you ask because you've had choices, son," he told me. "Me, I was taken to the colors as a boy of ten. I've known the army as mother and father. I met my wife in service, and I buried her last winter in New York. Now the army's my wife and my sweetheart, too, I suppose. I'm thirty-four years old, but I look forty-five, don't I? And from the feel of things, I'm not apt to reach that higher figure. When

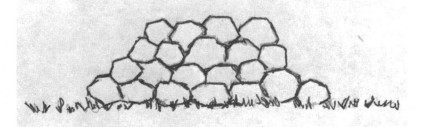

burial cairn

you're as old as I am now and doing something different, remember the old British sergeant you met on the Camden battlefield. Your name?"

"Francis Livingstone," I explained.

"Francis, my boy, you brought water day before yesterday to a young fifer. Do you recall the boy?"

"Yes," I said, trying not to remember his haunting eyes.

"If my Agnes and I had been blessed with a son, I would have prayed for him to be like Jeremiah. He was as fine and spry a lad as ever took to the parade ground. The surgeons had already given him up for dead, but not you. You gave him water just like the others, even though the sight of him shook you to the bone. There are too many boys lying in holes hereabouts or hanging from trees. I've seen that Tory captain's work. Now I'm going to turn and walk yonder. You go the other way. Find a horse and ride as fast and far as you can. In another day's time the cavalry will be off hunting Gates. Best be gone before that."

"Sergeant?"

"Nothing more need be said, son. Take your chance. You won't likely have another."

"You'll be in trouble."

"Never you mind, son. Now go."

I gripped his hands and whispered, "Thank you." Then I ran.

6

*J*DON'T THINK ANYONE ever felt as alone as I did that afternoon, running away from the burial cairn and vanishing in the tall grass beyond. I had no notion of what to do or where to go. I was afraid of the Tories. But I was worried over leaving Grandma and Kate. Captain Jarvis might well blame them for my escape. In the end, my worry overcame my fear. I returned to the tavern.

I hardly recognized the place. Surgeons were using the porch as a makeshift hospital. Inside, officers tried to drink away their misery. General Cornwallis had ordered sentries posted, but they were walking about a quarter mile from town. I easily slipped past them and made my way to the back door. I opened the door a crack and peered inside. I saw no one, so I crept inside and began searching for Grandma.

We saw each other at the same instant. Her eyes clouded over with fear, and she excused herself from serving a pair of colonels and hurried to my side.

"Child, you shouldn't be here," she scolded me. "That Captain Jarvis turned the tavern upside down only an hour ago, looking for you. What have you done to make them so angry?"

"It doesn't take much," I answered. "I gave George and some others water. I suppose it was foolish, but I couldn't help myself."

"I would have done the same," Grandma confessed. "But they're not hanging old women. Not at the moment, anyway. I'll get some food ready, but you have to leave. It's not safe for you here. Go north. You may find friends up there. But unless you're certain, avoid people altogether."

"What about you?" I asked.

"The colonels like the way I cook," she explained. "They won't let the feelings of a Tory captain cheat them out of a good dinner."

"And Kate?"

"That could be a problem," Grandma said, frowning. "A young lieutenant took her for a walk. She's late returning."

"I'll find her," I promised.

"You had best stay hidden," Grandma argued. "Kate can take care of herself."

A month before, I would have agreed. But the fighting had changed the temper of everyone, even the disciplined English officers. Some of them had turned mean, and I didn't trust my sister's welfare to them.

Despite Grandma's pleading, I stepped back outside. The town was full of sleeping and wounded soldiers. It was no place to take a pretty girl for a walk. And I was sure to be discovered if I searched for Kate there. I set off instead in the direction of the river. A quarter mile down the path George and I had traveled a hundred times, I heard something. Taking a deep breath, I left the path and hid behind a nearby oak. As my eyes adjusted to the darkness, I made out two shadowy figures just ahead. One wore the cocked hat of a British officer. The other was Kate. She was fending off the arms of the lieutenant.

I'm not exactly sure what possessed me next. Kate was holding her own, after all, and I was forty pounds lighter than the lieutenant, and unarmed. I grabbed a fallen branch, though. Solid oak makes a good club. Kate caught a glimpse of me as I raised my branch. She jerked free. The lieutenant never saw me. I slammed my branch down, splintering it against his neck and shoulders. He stumbled forward, and I hit him again. The branch struck the back of his head with a thud, and he fell to his knees, groaning. Kate gave him a good kick in the side and whacked his left ear. He fell on his face, moaning.

"Francis, is that you?" she asked as I took her hand.

"You know anyone else foolish enough to save you from the British?" I asked.

"I was saving myself just fine," she objected. "Now we're both in trouble."

"You know about it?" I asked.

"Half the Tory cavalry is looking for you. Now you'll have the British out, too."

"Well, I'm sure you would have managed it better," I growled. "I did the best I could. Sooner or later one of us

73

would have done or said something to get in trouble. Best we go now before Cornwallis seizes the whole state!"

"And Grandma?" she asked.

"She intends to stay."

"Doesn't want to slow us down, you mean," Kate said, sighing. "Well, I suppose you're right. Livingstones aren't known for walking softly among their enemies. I almost spilled a pot of tea on that Captain Jarvis when he began boasting how he would hang you from the nearest tree."

"If you had, I would probably have had company there," I told her. "Still might. It's a long way to the mountains."

"You think we should go home? I thought we might try for Uncle Hugh and Aunt Anne's place in North Carolina."

"Uncle Hugh's dead," I explained. "He was one of the ones I buried. John and Will, too. And with George a prisoner, I suspect Aunt Anne will have trouble enough without us adding to her burden."

"It's a long way, Francis," Kate reminded me. "And Joe's not along this time."

"I remember the way," I told her. "Maybe we can find our horses and—"

"I saw two Tories lead our horses through town," Kate said. "They've taken just about every animal in Kershaw County. It's a long walk."

"Too long," I said, swallowing hard. "We have to get horses. If the Tories stole ours, I guess we'll just have to steal a couple of theirs."

"Now that's a fine way to avoid trouble," Kate said. But

I could see her eyes sparking in the moonlight. I knew she would go along with the plan.

First, though, we returned to the tavern. Grandma provided us with a pair of blankets, a haversack filled with food, two wooden canteens, and my rifle. I could tell she was uncertain about handing over the gun. We stood a poor chance in a fight with Tory cavalry, and getting caught with a rifle was certain to get me hanged. We would need to hunt for food along the way, though, and I wouldn't have left Camden without it. I suppose she knew that. I couldn't imagine how I would have smuggled that rifle past dozens of British officers. Grandma managed it, though. She passed the rifle to me and smiled.

"Do your best to get past the pickets before daybreak," she whispered. "Kate, see he isn't reckless. Hide during daylight and move by night. It's the old way of the Scots, you know. The English hate the night, darlings. Try to be careful."

I hugged her tightly, and Kate kissed her cheek. She wasn't a big woman, but when she wrapped her arms around us, I feared we would never break free of that iron grip.

"We have to go, Grandma," Kate said. I nodded. She kissed us farewell. We hurried off past the cook shed and vanished into the woods. We were half a mile away before either of us dared to speak.

"Is that a tear?" I asked Kate as she rubbed her eyes.

"I got something in my eye," she grumbled.

"I'll miss Grandma, too," I told her. "But now we've got to find some horses."

"Yes," Kate agreed. "Best concentrate on the matter at hand."

Pa had said that a hundred times. I usually found some way to get distracted, though. Just then, with regiments of British soldiers camped all around us and Tories scouring the countryside, eager to stretch my neck, I couldn't afford to let my mind wander. I led the way to the river. There must have been two hundred horses grazing and drinking there. I located a fine white mare, but Kate shook her head.

"The darker the better," she urged. "Harder to see at night. Those two all alone, on the far side of the river, should do."

I nodded my agreement. They appeared well fed and rested. We took off our shoes and stockings. Kate lifted her skirts. Together we waded through the shallows of the Wateree River. Once across, we freed the horses from their hobbles and led them through a gap in the briers. I then returned, located saddle blankets, bridles, and saddles, and waited for the sentries to move along to another section of the river. Kate and I fetched what we needed, saddled our horses, and led them away from the river. Once the pinpricks of light made by the enemy campfires disappeared from sight, we climbed atop our mounts and headed northward. I gazed overhead at the North Star and felt it guiding us homeward. I silently prayed that God might watch over His poor vagabond children, for two of them were in dire need of divine protection just then.

I'm not sure how far we rode that night. Most of it was

along a fairly good road. I smelled the foul odor of the battlefield, and twice we stopped and led our horses around
British encampments. Only when I felt I would fall out of
the saddle did I call for Kate to halt. Her muffled answer
told me she was near to collapsing herself.

"Maybe those hills on the left," I said. "Not likely to be
any farms there."

"Nor many prying eyes," she agreed.

We left the road and headed across a cornfield toward
the hills. It seemed to take us forever, but it probably was
no more than a mile and a half. I located a burned patch
on the slope of the nearest hill and dismounted. I led my
horse to a natural corral formed by fallen logs and boul-
ders. We only had to close up the gap between lines of
stones. Best of all, a natural spring fed a small pool. I led
my horse inside, removed her saddle, and waited for Kate
to do the same. I then closed the corral by dragging two
fallen trees over. Leaving the horses to drink and chew the
soft grass of the hillside, I walked around in search of some
shelter. I located a small cave fifty yards from where we'd
left the horses. It made a perfect hideout.

Kate spread out our sleeping blankets a little way inside the cave, and I allotted us each half a cooked chicken
for supper. It would have tasted better warmed over a fire,
but I dared not chance it so close to Camden. Even inside
a cave, some light would emerge. It might be enough to
reveal us to our enemies. The chicken tasted quite fine
anyway, and we drank cup after cup of cool springwater. I
don't think I'd ever been as thirsty. Finally we lay on our

blankets. In the blink of an eye I was fast asleep.

I felt like I could have slept a month, but three hours later I was shaken awake by thunder. The sky darkened, and lightning crisscrossed the heavens. The rain came down in buckets, and we were wet to the skin even inside the cave. I fretted over our poor horses. But fearful and miserable as the storm made us, it proved a blessing. Any sign we had left along the way would be washed away, and no Tory patrols would depart Camden in that weather!

The Storm

We were still wet that night when we left the cave. The horses didn't much enjoy traveling, either. They were as wet as we were, after all, and I hated the notion of throwing soggy saddle blankets and damp leather saddles onto their backs. We had to put Camden behind us, though. I actually believe the horses sighed when we made camp in a clearing beside the Wateree a few hours before dawn. There was no cave this time, so I made us a shelter of branches topped by leaves and grass. We became nearly invisible as we slept through the daylight hours.

We continued our journey north and west in much the same fashion those next few days. Only once did we have a narrow escape, and even then it wasn't our fault. If Captain Jarvis was out looking for me, he apparently never believed me capable of traveling so far so fast. But there were other enemies for Cornwallis's cavalry to seek out. Colonels Sumter and Marion were raiding his supplies, and local bands of patriot militia skirmished with Tory neighbors.

An hour short of dusk during the final week of August, a ragged scarecrow of a boy came racing into our camp. We had concealed ourselves so well that he tripped over our saddles and fell headfirst into our shelter. Kate cried out, and I dashed from the horses to see what was the matter.

"Don't shoot!" the boy pleaded. "I'm nobody who'll cause you harm. If you're a friend of the king, I'm done for. If you're true to the cause of freedom, then you've found a friend and ally."

"You're safe enough," Kate declared. "We're no friends of the king."

"And he doesn't look like he sits down to dinner with any gentlemen," I said, examining his scratched and bloody bare legs and feet. His trousers were worn and so thin in places, they barely passed muster. His shirt was little more than a rag.

"I'm called Paul Keys," he explained. "I've ridden with Colonel Sumter some, but my brother Abner got himself killed at Camden, and I thought it best I go home and help Ma. Seems the neighbors heard and came looking for me. I've been afoot and running three days now. They're close behind!"

"Where's your rifle?" I asked.

"Friend, when five men on horseback are after you, you don't slow yourself down with anything. I fired my musket and flung it aside. I also had a fine German pistol, but I shot away my lead and hid it in some rocks. I hit one of those fellows, and another stayed behind with him. Three of them are coming this way, though."

"He led them right to us!" Kate exclaimed.

"Don't suppose he knew we were here," I pointed out. "Anyway, I don't hear horses."

"You will," Paul insisted. And the sound of hooves on the hard ground soon followed.

"What now?" Kate asked.

"Too late for running," I said, loading my rifle. My hands shook as I imagined firing on the Tories. Paul noticed.

"You couldn't shoot all three of them anyway," Paul argued. "Look, maybe we can discourage them. The colonel used this trick a time or two. If we spread out and stir up a lot of noise, maybe they'll imagine they've happened upon an army. They know I don't have a rifle, so if you space your shots here and there, they'll think we're a force to be reckoned with."

I turned to Kate, and she shrugged her shoulders. I didn't see another choice. Even if I managed to hit one rider, the other two would surely kill us. I hid behind a boulder. When the first rider appeared, I fired. I didn't hit, but they slowed their pursuit. Kate started shouting. Paul chirped in from down the hillside, and when I fired a second shot a hundred yards from where I'd taken my first, the three riders fled.

"Told you it would work," Paul said, forcing a smile onto his face. He then collapsed in a heap. Kate and I dragged him to our shelter and cleaned him up some. A sip of water brought him around.

"Build up a fire," Paul suggested. "No, three fires. Make it look like we're a company up here at least."

I nodded and set about doing just that. Kate cooked some wild onions and turnips. I'd shot a rabbit the day before, and we had what was left of it, too. Our dinner was no match for one of Grandma's stews, but it fended off our hunger until nightfall.

"We're headed to the mountains," I told Paul when we'd finished eating. "I'm sorry we can't spare you some clothes or food, but we've got little enough. You're not too big, though, so if you don't mind riding double, we can take you along with us a way. Maybe you can find yourself a horse."

"I appreciate the offer," Paul said, "but my home's near here. Once there, I'll have good shoes and clothes with no holes in them. Until then, I'll hope not to embarrass myself by sharing camp with any other pretty girls." He smiled at Kate, and she grinned back.

"We'll be leaving now it's dark," I explained.

"It's best," Paul agreed. "Don't worry. I know this country. I can circle around and lose those fellows in a bog. You've given me a chance to catch my breath. I'm grateful for it."

"Maybe we'll meet up again someday," Kate said.

"My place is on the road to Gilbert Town," Paul explained. "Next house south of the Grants. I'd welcome your visit."

Kate turned a little pale. She suddenly seemed vexed, and I couldn't imagine what had come over her. It wasn't until we were well clear of the camp that she told me.

"You remember the Grants," she said. "We stayed with them on the trip to Camden."

"Sure," I said.

"Well, they said their neighbors to the south were Tories. And now that I think about it, Keys was their name. It's just as well you didn't shoot anybody, Francis. Those were patriots chasing that boy."

"Well, what do you know?" I said, scratching my ear. "We fed a Tory."

"I don't half mind it, though," Kate said, laughing. "He was a pretty poor excuse for a boy, all scratches and tatters. No matter what his politics were, I don't believe he deserved to die."

"No," I said, remembering the British fifer. "There's been enough dying."

"If we've passed the Grants' place, we can't be far from Quaker Meadows," Kate said. "That's right, isn't it?"

"Less than a mile, as I remember it."

"And the British won't have come this far, will they?"

"Sure hope not," I confessed.

We nudged our horses into a trot and stared up ahead for some sign of life. I finally detected smoke rising from a chimney. It was Colonel McDowell's house, all right. We'd reached Quaker Meadows. Soon we would be among friends again. I felt a great weight lifted from my shoulders. I believed we were safe.

7

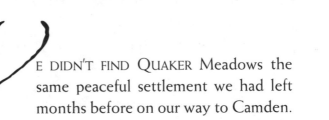

E DIDN'T FIND QUAKER Meadows the
same peaceful settlement we had left
months before on our way to Camden.
There were close to two hundred mili-
tia encamped there, most of them tired and hungry. With
them was a larger mass of women and children. Many of
them, like Kate and me, had fled their homes from fear of
the British and their Tory allies. Instead of being welcomed
as lost friends, we found ourselves an added burden to people who already had enough trouble.

As I stared at the encamped militia and tried to decide
what to do, I heard my name shouted.

"Why, it's Cherokee Frank and his renegade sister!"

I immediately rolled off my horse and turned in the
direction of the voice. My face reddened, and I was ready
for battle. Instead of some taunting enemy, though, I found
a laughing Joe O'Hara.

"Well, don't you have a word for an old friend?" he
called.

"You didn't sound all that friendly a minute ago," I answered.

"Well, I did get your attention," he said, laughing as he approached. He gripped my hands and waved to Kate. "I confess I gave you up for a ghost, Francis. We got news of the big battle at Camden, and I thought you'd surely be dead. How could so many British fail to shoot you?"

"Easy," I told him. "I wasn't a soldier. But that didn't save me long. I gave the prisoners water, and a Tory captain set out to hang me for it."

"Well, I'm glad you're not bending a tree," Joe said. "We need all the soldiers we can find now."

"I told you, Joe. I'm no soldier."

"You will be," he said. "It's one thing to stay home and look after your ma when the men set after the Cherokees. But when the enemy's marching into the mountains, promising to burn and kill anything he chooses, that's different."

"What?" I cried.

"Haven't you heard? Francis, you've come from Camden, haven't you? Don't you know that devil Tarleton's on the rampage? And a Scottish major, Pat Ferguson, is only days away, marching on Gilbert Town. He'll be here soon. And we're less than a week's march from the Watauga."

I wasn't quite prepared for so much news all at once, and my face showed it. Kate dismounted and put her hand to my forehead.

"Are you ill, Francis?" she asked.

"In a way," I said, sitting on the ground. I closed my eyes and tried to picture a map of our journey and the peril we hadn't even known about. Ferguson had close to a thousand Tories, many of them well-trained New Yorkers, approaching the border between South Carolina and North Carolina. Militia had fought one band of Tories after another in the mountain country, but none stood much chance against a trained and organized army led by a man like Ferguson or Tarleton. And now they were coming into the high country!

I opened my eyes and tried to recover my wits. Kate knelt beside me and squeezed my shoulders the way she had the day Charlie died. Joe forced a stupid grin onto his face.

"What are we to do?" I asked.

"Fight them before they reach our families," Joe declared. "Scare them the way they've scared us."

"And just how can a lot of farmers and woodsmen fight an army?" I asked. "You didn't see what a mess they made of us at Camden. You haven't seen Tarleton and his men. They hunger for killing the way a starving dog longs for a hog bone. You can't take people like these here," I said, waving my arms at the militia, "and challenge a thousand killers!"

"Sure, you can," Joe argued. "You can because you have to. The trick's to fight one batch at a time. Ferguson's closest, so we trap him first. Then we find the next bunch. As long as that English fellow Cornwallis scatters his folks here and there, we'll stand a chance."

I didn't believe him, though. He hadn't seen the British regiments with their fine uniforms and neat, clean rows of soldiers. He hadn't watched them march and drill. He hadn't seen the gleam of those bayonets or buried the pitiful dead who had crossed their paths.

I would have led Kate north toward home that very day, but she refused to leave.

"We're exhausted," she declared. "Joe says there's a detachment of soldiers going north in a few days. We can go with them."

"You mean they're leaving Quaker Meadows?" I asked. "They talk of fighting this Scottish major, but they're only running away."

"Whatever they're doing, we'll be safer with them than on our own," Kate insisted. It was hard to argue with that. So we remained at Quaker Meadows almost a week.

I did my best to provide for our needs. Each morning I went with Joe into the woods to hunt. We shot a deer the first day and shared our bounty with the others. Afterward, the best we managed was a rabbit or squirrel. It barely filled our bellies. Still, it was better than most of the hunters got. Game was growing scarce, and most of the crops were not ready for harvesting quite yet. The neighbor farms were short of cornmeal and sugar. The refugees were in need of everything. I wished we were on our way home.

When I wasn't hunting or fishing, I sat on a rock beside the river and sketched the surrounding mountains. Other times I improved the few sketches I'd made in Camden. I drew from memory the scenes of battle there, the red-headed Colonel Tarleton and the despicable Tory, Jarvis. While I was sketching one morning, a slender man in his thirties sat beside me and watched. I was drawing from memory the face of the British sergeant who had saved my life. It wasn't a good likeness. I didn't have the talent for capturing half-remembered faces with my pencil.

I set aside that drawing and began filling in some detail from an earlier drawing of Quaker Meadows.

"Been doing that long?" the man asked.

"Since midmorning," I explained. "I was fishing, but it seems like we've emptied the river hereabouts. Pa deems my drawing a waste of time, but I've really got nothing else to do."

He chuckled. "I meant drawing. Have you been doing it a long time? Years?"

"Since I can remember."

"You've got a fair eye for it," the man said. "I'm Joe McDowell. I understand you met my brother a few months back. I'm a major in the militia. What's left of it."

"Is it true the British are marching this way?" I asked.

"The scouts say Ferguson's at Gilbert Town," Major McDowell admitted. "Looks like we'll be going north tomorrow."

"There's no stopping them, is there?" I asked.

"Oh, we'll be stopping them," the major vowed. "We'll need help, though. It's coming from Georgia and Virginia. But we need to bring the overmountain boys, too. You're one yourself, I understand."

"I don't know that I could ever be a soldier, though."

"Oh? You've seen some fearful things, I suppose," he said as he peered at my various drawings.

"I'm not afraid," I insisted. "At least that's not all of it. It's just, well, I don't know that I could shoot another man."

"It's a hard thing, I agree. But someone's bound to do it. Otherwise, Ferguson and his Tories will do all the killing. We can't allow that. But you could help the army in another way."

"How?"

"Your drawing. You could ride ahead, with the scouts, and sketch the enemy camps. They can tell us what lies ahead, but you can show us. You needn't decide now. But soon I may ask you again. So start thinking about it."

"Thinking is something I *can* do," I told him.

The following morning, most of the gathering set off for the Watauga settlements. Kate and I went with them. Although it turned out that Ferguson wasn't on our heels, no one objected. Kate and I were excited at the prospect of seeing our family again. The refugees hoped for more assistance. And the soldiers expected help from their over-mountain friends.

It wasn't as easy climbing the mountains as coming down, and it took us the better part of a week to cross over Roan Mountain and descend into the valley of the Watauga. The others groaned and moaned as they rode or led their horses. The slopes were often steep, and the trails were narrow. I frequently carried a small boy or girl behind me, for the lowland folk couldn't seem to catch their breath in the mountains. Kate laughed at me, but she soon did the same. Joe O'Hara once had three little ones on his horse's back while he led the creature along the trail on foot.

Once we were free of the ridge and down in the valley itself, Kate and I split off from the mob and headed for home. Joe followed for a time before turning off toward his mother's cabin. We passed the Carter place and continued past Fort Caswell and the Moore house. As we approached our cabin, I felt a terrible emptiness. Suddenly I remembered how tall I had felt, heading to Camden with Kate. I was returning a refugee. I'd left Grandma behind, on her own. She didn't even have George to help her now.

"I need to stop," I told Kate. "I can't face Pa. He'll be mad."

"He won't," she argued. "Come on."

She slapped my horse's rump, and I had little choice but to continue. By the time I had my mare in hand, Jamie and Alek were racing toward us, shouting and waving their arms.

"Kate's back!" they yelled. "Francis is here!"

Ma appeared on the porch. She watched us with tears in her eyes, and when I dismounted, she raced over and hugged me tightly.

"We all thought you dead," she said, sobbing. She waved Kate closer and pulled her into our embrace.

"Why?" Kate asked.

"Your aunt Anne wrote," Ma explained. "Hugh and her boys were killed. We learned from others that you had left Camden. We've heard about the Tories. I prayed, but I

90

never expected both of you to return to me."

I felt her tears stain my shirt. I could also feel Jamie and Alek as they rested their heads against my chest. I believed they were crying, too.

"I'd better take care of the horses," I said at last. "They've had a hard ride."

"I'll do it," Jamie said, stepping away. He seemed a lot taller at twelve than I remembered. Well, he had been growing half a year since I'd seen him, hadn't he?

"I'll help," Alek added.

With my little brothers off taking care of the horses, I had a chance to kiss Ma's forehead and assure her we were fine.

"And George isn't dead, Ma," I told her. "He's a prisoner."

"Not anymore," Ma said, gripping my hands tightly. "He's signed his parole and promised to fight for the British."

"What?" I gasped.

"Don't hold it against him," Ma pleaded. "He did it to protect his mother and their home. The Tories would have burned everything. And what chance would George have had, rotting on one of those prison hulks in Charleston Harbor? None. None at all. Maybe the men can put a stop to Ferguson and end this war."

"It will take more than that," I grumbled.

"We have to start somewhere, though," Kate declared. "If *we* don't stand up to them, who will?"

I thought that was easy for her to say. No one expected *her* to shoulder a rifle and shoot people. But the look in her eye told me that she would willingly take her place in the line of battle and give the British or Tories a fight they wouldn't soon forget.

As the long lines of militia and refugees streamed along the river and collected at Sycamore Shoals, Kate helped our brothers tend to the hogs. I chopped wood. Ma would gladly have sat us down at the table and talked our ears off, but I welcomed the work. I thought that perhaps if Pa saw me splitting firewood, he would be less disappointed in me for fleeing Camden. But as I chopped and chopped, he didn't appear. Finally, exhausted, I set the ax aside, stacked the wood beside the cabin, and stumbled inside.

"You're worn-out," Ma complained. "I told you not to stay out there too long."

I just sighed and slumped in a chair. That was when Pa stepped inside.

"You're back," he said, appearing surprised.

"Oh, Pa," Kate said, wrapping her arms around him. "I missed you so."

"Was your grandmother well when you left?" Pa asked. Although Kate was beside him, he looked to me for the answer.

"She was well," I said, "but I wish she'd come with us. Those Tories might turn on her."

"You might have remained to protect her," Pa said.

"He couldn't," Kate declared. "A Tory captain was after him. Me, too. We couldn't stay. I think Grandma was afraid she would slow us down. And besides, George was a prisoner in Camden."

"Don't you believe your brother can speak for himself?" Pa said, eyeing Kate harshly.

"I'm the oldest," she answered. "Besides, Francis is spent from splitting logs. He saved my life more than once, Pa."

"Yes?" he asked.

I stared at my toes and shook my head. "Not really," I said.

I expected him to say something, but he didn't. In fact, he hardly spoke. Afterward, he chatted with my brothers, and he insisted Kate relate our adventures. But he couldn't seem to look me in the eye. I sighed and began sketching.

I didn't have a chance to speak with him the following morning, either. The leading men of the valley had gone to discuss what to do about the invading British. I went about my chores as if I had never gone anywhere. There was plenty to do. Pa had only just begun harvesting our corn crop. With him off at the meeting, it was up to Jamie, Alek, and me to collect the ears in a wagon and transport them to the cribs.

"It's a poor trade," Alek announced. "The three of us don't make up for Pa."

That afternoon, when Kate finished helping Ma with the weekly washing, she joined us. Even Ma came out for a time.

It turned out that we had plenty of help with the harvest. For a share of the crop, the refugee families joined in the work. Ma welcomed their aid.

"We would have shared our corn anyway," she told us. "This way the people won't feel beholden to us."

Harvest was usually a joyful time, but the threat of the invading British hung over us like a thundercloud. The storm was sure to come, and we all knew it. When the last of the corn was safely in a crib, the men announced their plan to march back across the mountains and fight that Ferguson and his men before they had a chance to cause any more harm.

Colonels Isaac Shelby and John Sevier began enlisting men by the dozens to fill their militia regiments. Colonel Shelby had won a fine reputation defeating the Tories at a place called Musgrave Mill, and there were plenty of Wataugans eager to follow him south. Colonel Sevier had done most of his fighting in the mountains, chasing Cherokees and Shawnees from the settlements. Pa had served with him twice and deemed him a cool head in a fight. Charles McDowell and his brother Joe, who had led the exodus from Quaker Meadows, added recruits to their little command. When Col. William Campbell's Virginians arrived, over a thousand fighting men gathered that September afternoon.

I watched as Pa stepped up and signed his name to Colonel Sevier's muster. All my old doubts remained, and my feet seemed glued to the ground. Then Josh Moore followed his father and signed the list. Joe O'Hara also enlisted. Others stared at me. I shut my eyes and remembered the carnage at Camden. But I also recalled George's forlorn face and my cousins' lifeless bodies. I imagined Alek and Jamie likewise struck down, Ma driven from her cabin, and my friends all herded as prisoners to Charleston.

"Hard to decide, eh?" Major McDowell asked, resting a heavy hand on my shoulder. "Remember what I said to you? We could use you."

I took a deep breath and let it out slowly. I glanced around, hoping to locate Pa. He was nowhere to be seen.

"I guess I could draw maps without having to shoot anyone," I said.

"Sooner or later a man has to shoulder his rifle," the major added. "You can't expect your enemies to be charitable. And it's not fitting to expect your friends to do your fighting."

"I suppose not," I said, frowning. I then set my feet in motion. When I arrived before Colonel Sevier, one of his brothers handed me a quill pen. I dipped it in an inkwell and signed my name carefully: *Francis Hugh Livingstone.*

I stepped away from the table. I was prepared to go home and begin readying my belongings. Each of us was to bring back a horse, a rifle, and enough food to last several days. I also planned to pack a blanket and the canteen Grandma had given me. Before I could move toward our cabin, though, two hands gripped my shoulders like the claws of an iron eagle. I glanced up into Pa's angry eyes.

"What do you think you're doing?" he growled. "I look away a moment, and you're joining the army!"

"I thought it's what you would want," I told him.

"When did I ever tell you that? Francis, how can I leave your mother and brothers with no one to look after them?"

"Pa, if I had been in Camden, you still would have signed the muster."

"I would have made arrangements with Levi Moore or Ed Smith or someone to stay and watch over the farm. Now what am I to do?"

"It's too late for me to stay, Pa."

"No, it's not," he argued. "I know John Sevier. It's a simple enough thing to scratch off a name. No one will think less of you for it."

"They will, too, Pa. Most everyone. I can't say I can blame them, either, not with every other boy in the valley marching."

"You're sure you want to do this?" Pa asked.

"No, but I don't suppose you're all that happy to leave home yourself."

"Never am," he said, nodding solemnly. "Francis, there's a part of me that's truly proud of what you're doing. Most of me is very worried, though."

"Sir?" I asked, confused.

"There's always been a wall between us, Francis, but you can't believe I'm eager to put you in danger." My eyes told him otherwise. He frowned. "When it comes time for fighting, you stay close and don't take chances. Understand?"

"I'll try," I answered. "But from what I know about battles, nothing turns out like you plan it."

"You keep talking like that, son, we'll have to appoint you a general. You make more sense than that fool Gates!"

He laughed, but I could tell that underneath he was worried. I knew that he was thinking about Ma, Kate, and my brothers, but there was a moment or two when his sad eyes fixed themselves entirely on me. And I suppose he was thinking some about Charlie, too. We walked together along the river to our cabin.

If Pa was bothered by the notion of me joining the militia, Ma was downright angry.

"You've just gotten home!" she exclaimed. "I can't imagine you want to leave again!"

"It's expected," I told her.

"Not by me," she declared, staring deeply into my eyes. "I know my son, don't I? You can't be doing this because you want to."

"Maybe not," I said, gazing at my feet. "But I have to go just the same. I can't let them march up here and hurt you. I can't let them—"

"And I suppose you'll tell me that one fourteen-year-old boy is going to make a difference?"

"I don't know. But if I stay behind when Josh and the others go, when will I ever belong here in this valley?"

"Fighting a battle won't change that," she argued.

"Standing with the others might," I answered. "I don't know if I'll be any use at all in a fight, Ma. But Major McDowell says I could ride ahead with the scouts, draw what I see. How many times have you told me it was a gift, my drawing? Maybe this is why that gift came to me."

She sighed.

"You're so much like your father," she grumbled. "You two don't remember fifty lines of Scripture, but you certainly know when to turn it against me. I can't argue with those sentiments, and you know it. Francis, I can't believe it's God's will to take my second son from me. I'm not Job! I could never bear such a sorrow."

She rested her head on my shoulder and wept. I'd never felt her shudder the way she did at that moment. And her tears never flowed as they did then—not even when Charlie died.

"I need to gather my things," I finally announced.

"Yes," she said, releasing me. "I suppose I've got work to do myself."

Pa joined her then. They exchanged a few harsh words before growing quiet and solemn.

"I'll look after him, dear," Pa promised. "I'll see he comes to no harm."

"It's not a promise you can keep," she insisted. "I'm certain Hugh told Anne the same thing. A British bayonet is no respecter of vows."

A terrible gloom settled over our cabin the rest of the afternoon. Pa and I cleaned our rifles. Then, while he walked off to talk with Kate and my brothers, I split logs so there would be plenty of firewood to last until we returned. I was still splintering lengths of pine when Kate motioned that it was time for supper.

"Already sick of the valley?" she asked as I washed my hands and face.

"You know better than most why I have to go," I replied.

"I know why you're going," she agreed. "Doesn't make any sense, but I know your reasons. I guess you think you've been gone half a year already, so nobody's going to miss you."

"I'm not that stupid," I told her.

"No?" she asked. "Seems so to me."

"Don't argue with me, Kate," I said, forcing a smile onto my face. "I don't think I could stand it. If you were a boy, you'd be marching with Pa. Charlie would. Isn't it time I should be what everybody expects?"

"No," she told me. "Charlie would be older. I am. If you were seventeen or so, it would be different. You're not. And fool that you are, you may never get to be seventeen, either. I always thought Charlie was rash for trying to ride that horse, but he seems almost sensible compared to you."

"You saw those Tories, Kate," I said, fighting off the memories of Camden. "And the British. They're coming here next. We have to stop them before that."

"And you're going to shoot them, are you? You can barely muster the meanness to fire on a rabbit, Francis Livingstone! How are you going to kill a man?"

I had no answer for her. And even though Major McDowell had said I would be sketching the Tory camps, I knew there was more to soldiering than drawing pictures.

I followed Kate inside. We sat together on one side of the table. Pa said a prayer, and we began eating. Truth was, I had little appetite. Ma had baked a ham, and we had roasted ears of sweet corn and a pot of beans to go with it. I just nibbled at a slice of ham and chewed a few beans. I did eat an ear of corn.

After supper, Ma began making balls of cornmeal for us to carry in our provision bags. There was plenty of jerked meat for us to take, too.

"Come here, Francis," she called to me when she had put the last of the cornmeal balls into a Dutch oven to bake.

"Ma?" I asked.

"That shirt will never last you," she said, poking a finger through a hole in the gingham shirt Grandma had given me at Camden. "The trousers are fine, but I think you'll need this."

She pulled a good hunting shirt made of soft doeskin from a trunk and placed it against my chest.

"Take your shirt off," she instructed. "Let's see how it fits."

I unbuttoned my shirt and let it drop to the floor. Ma then draped the hunting shirt over my head and let it take shape on my bony shoulders.

"There's room for some growing in this one," she said, nodding. "Tsula left it for you. He worried he might not be back before you needed it."

"He wasn't," I observed.

"Francis, don't grow so much I don't recognize you," she said, hugging me tightly.

"We don't either of us have much say about that, do we?" I whispered.

That night I lay in my bed with Jamie and Alek, wondering whether I'd made the right choice. There really hadn't been any choosing, though. I'd done what was expected of me. I couldn't claim to be fearless. I was plenty afraid. But it was like that first hunt. I couldn't allow Pa to do all the hard things anymore.

* * *

We didn't set off directly for Gilbert Town. It was a tradition in the mountains to mark a bountiful harvest with a revival. That year we deemed it particularly important to seek spiritual assistance for our little army. The Reverend Samuel Doak, a tall, white-haired preacher known far and wide, called all the people together at Sycamore Shoals. We soldiers went ready to march. Our families came to pray for our safety and success.

Nobody who was there forgot our revival that year. Reverend Doak was inspiring. He must have been seventy years old that autumn. The wind blew his wild white hair, and his booming voice echoed up and down the valley as if God Himself were speaking. He chose his words well.

Ma had taught us early to read the Bible. After all, she was a preacher's daughter. We recited verses every Sunday. I'd never heard the passages Reverend Doak used before, though. The kind, forgiving God that Ma told us about seemed to have changed into a vengeful power. We were urged to lift up our swords and smite our enemies.

"When I blow with a trumpet, I and all that are with me, then blow yet the trumpets also on every side of all the camp and say, 'The sword of the Lord, and of Gideon.'"

There were cries of "Amen" and echoes of "the sword of the Lord, and of Gideon." Even little boys shook fists toward the imagined British army hurrying northward. As for the rest of us, we gritted our teeth and imagined ourselves marching toward the towering walls of Jericho.

I don't think another man alive could have filled the valley with such fury. We were shouting and praying and threatening our enemies with pure passion. In truth, I wasn't certain the whole gathering wouldn't follow us southward.

I waited for Pa to say his final farewells before I spoke my own. I hugged Ma and Kate and promised again not to be foolish.

"Don't you get yourself killed," Ma said, holding on to my hands.

"I'll miss your antics," Kate said, leading me toward the river. "You'll come back, hear? I won't sleep unless you promise me."

"I'll do my best," I answered. "I'm in no hurry to get killed."

Last of all, I sat with Jamie and Alek while the colonels began organizing their men.

"Take care of things, won't you?" I said.

"We'll do what we can," Jamie said, holding my hand a moment. "We're not ready to do it all yet, though. You've got to come back and help with spring planting."

"If I don't, it won't get done," I answered. "You two always manage to get lost down at the river when it's time to start the plowing."

"And who taught us that trick?" Alek asked.

I grinned and drew them close. "But you'll manage it if I'm a little longer returning than we expect."

"Sure," Jamie agreed.

"Don't worry about us," Kate said, lifting Alek's chin. "We're Livingstones. We always do what's necessary, remember?"

"Sure," I agreed.

Pa collected me then. We walked slowly, silently, to where our horses were tethered. I climbed into my saddle. Pa did likewise. Then we joined the others. I doubted that I would ever be able to shoot anyone, but I planned to do everything else I could to help defeat our enemies. I didn't have Gideon's sword, but I had my Dickert rifle. I prayed that would be enough.

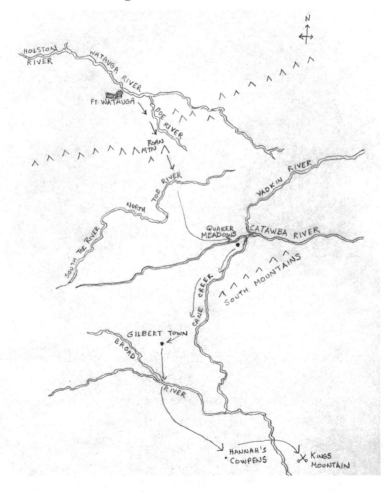

8

*I*FOLLOWED PA TOWARD Roan Mountain, but I didn't stay with him long. Major McDowell appeared and ordered Joe O'Hara and me forward. We were to ride ahead with the scouts. Pa was none too happy about the idea.

"I know that country better than either of these boys," he objected. "Let them stay here with the main force."

"People are accustomed to seeing young O'Hara riding about," the major explained. "And Francis here can draw us a picture of what we're facing. I've got a couple of good men to lead the way. Don't worry. We won't let them come to any harm. We want information, not a fight. And they're not the only scouts we're sending. We'll have a couple of dozen men out. But I'd put my money on these youngsters. It's said Ferguson's made Gilbert Town his headquarters, and nobody knows that town better than Matthew Lewis."

I gave Pa a confused glance. He waved me on, and I followed Major McDowell and Joe along the line of horsemen until we met up with two raggedy-looking fellows.

"Meet Amos Weaver and Lieutenant Matt Lewis," the major said. "The poorest excuses for men that I know. But they're good at finding Tories."

The shorter of the two, a beardless boy not much older than Joe and I, waved.

"That's my cousin Amos," a barrel-chested man with the stubble of a beard announced. "We're from Gilbert Town. Know everybody for miles around. Aren't many Tories there, and even they get along with us."

"Good to know," Joe said. "I'm Joe O'Hara. This scrawny youngster's Francis Livingstone. Neither one of us has any idea what we're supposed to do. You boys will have to tell us."

"Don't worry yourselves a bit about that," Amos said, laughing. "Matt's a natural-born general. He's half snake, too, so he knows every hole for miles around. If there's trouble, he'll find us a hiding place."

"We're not in the army to hide," Joe objected.

"Well, no four men alive are going to stand up to a hundred Tories, and Ferguson's got ten times that many," Matt said, waving us along. "A scout hides when he needs to. He runs when he needs to. He only fights when there's no choice. Or when his colonel deems it prudent."

And so we four rode out ahead of the others. It seemed as if Joe, Kate, and I had ridden the trail to Roan Mountain just days before. Everything still looked peaceful. The trees were showing a tinge of orange and yellow. The army camped on the mountain that night. We passed the summit and traveled another ten miles before stopping. It proved a blessing because it snowed heavily that night. Cold as we were on the eastern slope, I hated to imagine how Pa and my friends in their camp near the summit must have suffered. We enjoyed better weather thereafter, and we arrived at Quaker Meadows on the third day. We were considerably ahead of the army by then. Although we heard much talk about Ferguson and his army, we didn't spot a trace of them along the way.

In truth, I felt pretty useless. There was no enemy army to sketch, and I passed most of the day with Joe, shooting rabbits or waiting for word from Matt or Amos. They had ridden ahead. I would have been content to stay with the Grants and allow Matt and Amos to locate Ferguson. Fate didn't seem to pay any mind to my wants those days, though. Matt returned with news that a party of Ferguson's green-shirted New Yorkers was on the road five miles ahead. Joe and I mounted our horses and followed our companions southward.

I'd heard Matt tell us more than once that scouts should stay hidden and watch. He didn't seem to be doing either, though. We rode recklessly on the road, in plain sight, for anybody to see. Only as the sun set did Matt show a trace of caution. He led us to a rocky hillside and showed us a good hiding spot beside a bubbling spring. It offered a fine view of the road, and we had cover if any Tories came looking for us.

None did. We didn't make a fire, and I slept fitfully. It had turned cold in the South Mountains, and I'd had only cold cornmeal to eat that night. It didn't appear likely that

I would enjoy anything better in the coming days.

I was used to rising early, but weary as I was, I slept well past dawn that next morning. I might have slept the whole day had not Joe finally roused me. He had a worried look on his face, and I rubbed the sleep from my eyes.

"What's wrong?" I asked.

"Ask him," Joe suggested, pointing to Amos.

"Where's Matt?" I asked, noticing there were only three of us left in our little camp.

"Gone ahead," Amos explained.

"Tell him," Joe urged.

"He's ridden on to Gilbert Town," Amos added. "A rider passing by said Ferguson was rounding up local families, taking their horses and cows, burning their houses, and even hanging some of the men. My pa's been dead three years now, and Ma's safe in the mountains with your people. My brothers and little sister, too. Matt's ma and two brothers are still at home, near Gilbert Town. You can't blame him for wanting to make sure they're safe."

"And how's he going to do that all alone?" Joe asked. "Would have been best if the four of us went together. Now what are we to do? Go ahead? What if he comes back and we're hunting for him? Fine scouts we are, splitting up, forgetting our job."

"You better ride back and warn the others," I told Joe.

"Why me?" he asked.

"You've got the best horse," I pointed out. "You know every inch of that trail. Amos and I can go ahead, see if we can find Ferguson. Then I can make a drawing of the town and mark where the pickets are posted. It's why I came, remember?"

"You taking charge now?" Amos asked.

"No, but somebody should. If you've got a better plan, I'm listening."

"Don't," Amos admitted. "What do you think, Joe?"

"I don't like it, but I guess it's as good a notion as any. Francis, don't go getting yourself killed now. I don't have so many friends I can afford to lose one. Besides, Kate would never forgive me. I promised to look after you."

"What?"

"She was half of a mind to come along," Joe said, shaking his head. "As if we don't have enough distractions already." He laughed, and a little of my fear drifted away. It returned as soon as he departed.

Amos and I started for Gilbert Town. He figured we had twenty-five miles to go. It was two or three days riding at an easy pace, but we hurried ourselves and cut the trip to a day and a half. We stayed off the road and used every shortcut Amos knew. We lit no fires and hardly ate anything along the way. We stopped mainly to rest the horses.

Perhaps three miles shy of Gilbert Town, I spied a column of smoke to my right. Amos grew alarmed the instant he saw it. He turned in that direction, and I followed. I would gladly have waited for daybreak before venturing so close to the settlement, but Amos seemed determined to run the risk. I figured I was better off with him than on my own.

I don't think I'll ever forget the sight of that burned cabin. Only half the chimney remained, and the barn and cook shed were just dark scars on the rocky earth. Amos was standing beside a well, holding the reins of his horse. I circled around past him and had a good look. The place seemed deserted. Back of the barn, there was a mound of fresh-turned earth, though.

"This is Matt's place," Amos explained. "And that's a grave. You think those Tories killed all of them? Nathan wasn't but twelve years old! Zachary's fifteen now. He might have gone with us, but he was worried about leaving his ma alone."

"What about Matt's father?" I asked.

"He was with General Lincoln at Charleston," Amos told me. "Nobody knows what's become of him."

"What do you want to do?" I asked.

"Joe told me you're part Cherokee."

"Mostly my hair and eyes," I said, scratching my chin. "Why's that matter?"

"Because I think we should leave the horses in that stand of willows there. We go ahead slow and careful, like Indians, quiet and as close to invisible as we can make ourselves. Understand?"

"You mean go all the way to Gilbert Town?"

"We don't know where Matt's gone, Francis. He may have ridden into that town, shooting and screaming like a banshee. If he did, he's dead."

"And we're the only ones left to find out if Ferguson's still here with his army."

"Would seem so," Amos said, yawning. "I'd rather know before nightfall, too."

And so we did just what Amos said. We silently wove our way from tree to tree. We had our rifles, but we knew they would offer us a poor chance in a fight. Even if we shot a picket or two, there would be dozens of Tories rushing at us a moment later. Besides, nervous as I was, I doubted I could hit a wagon, much less a man. Even if I'd wanted to!

By the time we reached the scattered buildings that formed the little village of Gilbert Town, it was dusk. You couldn't tell how much of an army was camped in and around the town, but I counted more than thirty cook fires. We didn't see Ferguson himself, but there was a band of men in green coats. Several men walked around, issuing orders.

"Officers," Amos whispered. "It's them for certain."

I couldn't really see well enough to make a proper sketch, and there were two pickets not twenty yards away.

Gilbert Town

Amos deemed that too close for safety. He tapped my shoulder and motioned toward a deserted corral. We were nearly there when the sound of laughter attracted our attention. I glanced back into Gilbert Town in time to see a barrel-chested fellow with a familiar voice slap the back of one of those green-coated Tories.

"Can't be," I said quietly. "He's gone over to the enemy, Amos."

"Shhh," Amos replied. "Come on."

I followed Amos to the corral. He then let me know what he thought of my notion.

"Sometimes a scout tracks the enemy," Amos explained. "Sometimes he's got to go down among them and find out what's afoot."

It sounded like a dangerous game to me, and I wanted no part of it. Amos insisted we stay near town, though. We burrowed our way into the hillside and disguised ourselves with leaves. Then Amos went to sleep. I tried, but every snapping twig or hooting owl drove nails of fear into my heart. I didn't get much rest.

As the first traces of dawn streaked a cloudy sky, I shook myself to life and went to work. Major McDowell wanted drawings, and I would give him some. I drew the store and tavern, the farmhouses and fences. I then put little dots in to represent the Tories. I marked each cook fire with an x. By the time Amos woke, I was halfway finished. He crawled off to have a look around. When he returned, he pointed out the picket posts and located two other camps of Tories.

"I think we ought to go back to Matt's place now," he declared when I finished my drawing. "We can fetch our horses and find a place to watch the road. If Matt's got any sense at all, he'll be leaving Gilbert Town by midday."

"If they let him," I added.

"Well, if he's not along by then, it's best we ride north without him. We need to tell the colonels what they're up against."

I nodded my agreement. Once again, we quietly wove our way through the trees the three miles to Matt's burned home. When we approached the place, though, my nostrils picked up the scent of something beside charred logs. It was bacon! And johnnycakes.

Amos raced ahead and practically jumped out of the trees when he saw his aunt flipping johnnycakes in her big cast-iron skillet. A boy about Alek's shape and size was feeding sticks to the fire.

"My stars!" Mrs. Lewis exclaimed. "Is that you, Amos?"

"Aunt Maggie!" Amos said, wrapping his arms around her. "Nathan!"

The boy brightened some at the sight of his cousin.

I didn't really want to interrupt their reunion, but the scent of cornmeal crackling in bacon fat was more than my stomach could resist. I stumbled out of the trees.

"Ma!" Nathan cried in alarm.

Mrs. Lewis reached for a rifle, but Amos snatched it away.

"He's a friend," Amos explained.

"A hungry one, I suspect," Mrs. Lewis said, studying my face. "When did you boys last eat?"

"Chewed a bit of corn bread yesterday," I told her.

"Haven't had meat in days," Amos declared. "Been afraid to make a fire. Now yours is burning, though, I can't see not taking advantage of something hot."

"Come along and warm yourselves, children," Mrs. Lewis said. Amos and I sat on the opposite side of the fire as she finished cooking. After we ate, she told us the saddest tale I'd ever heard.

I'd always considered war a foolish thing. Throughout the fighting with the Cherokees, I worried one side or the other of my family would come to grief. As for the bigger war with the king of England's armies, I'd seen enough of it at Camden to last me.

The war we were fighting now, though, was pure crazy. Neighbor was fighting neighbor. Friends were killing friends. People on both sides burned houses and killed people for seemingly no reason at all.

When Major Ferguson had arrived at Gilbert Town, a couple dozen families had ridden to town to welcome him. They also swore their loyalty. Some of the men joined Ferguson's army. And some of them handed over lists of patriot families. One of those lists had Matt's name on it, but he, of course, was riding with Major McDowell. A dozen riders came to the Lewis farm. When they couldn't locate Matt, they dragged his brother Zachary out instead.

"He was scarcely five feet tall," Mrs. Lewis said through a sea of tears. "First they whipped his back raw. Then they put a noose around his neck and hanged him from that tall oak there. When he quit struggling, they laughed and joked."

"Then they burned our house," Nathan added. "And the barn. They stole our horses. They butchered the hogs and drove off the cows. Left us with nothing."

George had told me weeks before that once I got mad enough, I'd be able to kill. I guess I was about as mad as it was possible to get at that moment. Amos was too sad to voice his fury. I wasn't. I got to my feet, grabbed my rifle, and stared hard toward Gilbert Town.

"Don't even consider it," Mrs. Lewis warned. "Don't you think I want to punish those who killed my son? But I've got Nathan to worry over. And Matthew. I've given more than a woman should have to give. And I may have to give more. You boys, too. But the four of us are like gnats to that demon Ferguson. You get word to Colonel Campbell's men. Bring Shelby's boys down from the mountains. Then we'll settle with Ferguson!"

"Yes, ma'am," I answered.

She fried up some extra johnnycakes for us to take along and gave us bacon, too. Amos then said a sad farewell to his aunt. We collected our horses and headed for the road. Amos led the way to a rocky ridge where we concealed our horses and ourselves. There we waited.

It was a little after noon when Matt Lewis appeared on the road. Amos leaped up onto a boulder and drew his cousin's attention. Matt turned his horse toward us and whipped it into a gallop. Finally, the three of us were together again.

"Look," Matt said, handing over a large sheet of paper. It was a proclamation of Ferguson's intentions. If anyone

114

doubted whether the war had come to the mountains, he could doubt it no longer. The Scottish major had named Colonels McDowell and Shelby in particular, and he called us all little better than dogs intent on befouling the country.

"We're not the ones riding around, hanging boys and burning barns!" Amos said angrily.

I didn't know about any patriots hanging boys, but I'd heard plenty of stories in Camden about houses and barns torched by both sides. Amos's remark drew a wild look from Matt, and the cousins went off alone and talked. Then Matt mounted his horse and rode away.

"I thought we were heading north!" I complained.

"You can't blame Matt for wanting to see his ma and brother," Amos answered. "We're going on. He'll catch up soon enough."

"If it were me, I wouldn't leave them here alone," I said.

"You're not Matt. And you don't know Aunt Maggie. Besides, Matt says Ferguson's not staying here long. We'd best bring the others along quickly. It wouldn't do for the mouse to run away before the cat pounces. Gilbert Town's a fine place for a fight. We can come out of the woods and catch them napping."

"And if they leave?"

"Then we scouts will have to find them, Francis. And we might just be the mouse that gets caught."

9

ATT REJOINED US ON the road, and we continued north together. Fortunately, Joe had gotten word to the army, and we encountered a party of horsemen before nightfall. "The rest are on their way," Major McDowell told us. "Won't be long now."

It seemed long. We made camp a day's march short of Gilbert Town and waited. And waited. When the army finally arrived, it seemed to have lost its heart. I wished Reverend Doak had come along to breathe some fire into us. The hard ride over the mountains and across the rivers had disheartened many men. I was cheered by the news that more Virginia militia had arrived. The others seemed more concerned by rumors they'd heard at Quaker Meadows about British reinforcements.

There was considerable talk of returning home. Joe told me one of the Virginians said that Cornwallis had his whole army at Charlotte. Rumors about Tarleton were making their way through the ranks, too. Fighting

Ferguson's Tories was one thing. Nobody wanted to face the entire British army!

To make matters worse, the colonels began arguing about who was to command the army. And while they were debating what to do, the weather turned sour. It rained most of October 2. The men remained in camp the following morning, trying to dry themselves and their equipment.

Part of me was glad of the delay. Major McDowell sent a handful of men to keep an eye on Gilbert Town. Joe and I rode into Colonel Sevier's camp and rejoined our neighbors. I greeted Pa with a smile and a wave, and he motioned me to his side. He'd never been a man to show his emotions, but he squeezed my shoulder and led me aside. He seemed like a different man.

"What do you think of soldiering?" he asked.

I turned and studied the mob cluttering the road. There were a few more than a thousand of them altogether. Except for carrying rifles, they didn't look much like soldiers. After Camden I knew the difference.

"Soldiering?" I said, scratching my chin. "Is that what we're doing? I feel more like we're hunting a skunk."

Pa laughed. "Does remind you of it, doesn't it?" he asked. "You rush after the critter. Then, when you get close, you wonder if catching it's really worth the consequences."

I laughed at the thought.

"Come on," Pa urged. "Bet we've got a kettle boiling. You wouldn't turn down a hot cup of tea, would you?"

"No, sir," I answered.

I found myself surprisingly welcome in Colonel Sevier's camp. Men and boys who had taunted me for years listened eagerly as Joe and I told of spying on Ferguson. There were sorrowful eyes when Joe told of Matt's dead brother and burned home. Each of us knew the same fate might be awaiting our own families.

"You've done well," Mr. Moore told me. "To be truthful, I had my doubts that you would hold up under the hardships. You've always been full of surprises, though, Francis."

"Did you see their bayonets?" Josh asked after his father left. "I'm not afraid of a musket ball, but I have nightmares about being stabbed to death by bayonets. It's how Tarleton's men killed those Virginians at the Waxhaws."

"I've seen bayonets," I answered. "And I've seen Tories. They're just men, Josh. They're fierce killers of boys and hogs, I hear. I'm neither."

Later, Pa warned me to take more care with my answers.

"Josh is nervous, son," Pa said. "It's right that he should be afraid. I hope you are."

"Sir?"

"We've got too many youngsters in this army. A boy ought to have a few hairs on his chin before he gets shot."

"Maybe," I answered. "Just seems to a lot of us that the Tories don't care whether you've used a razor or not. They're hanging short little fellows down near Camden just because their fathers are in the militia. Pa, they were sure to do something unpleasant to me if I'd stuck around. All I did was give water to some prisoners."

"You don't know what battles are about," Pa said, gripping my arms in his fingers. "It's nothing short of murder, Francis. I've seen men who've shot bears drop their rifles and run. And I've watched boys get themselves split open with a war ax."

"It's not any better when they're older, is it?"

"Better? Maybe not. Different, though. Look around at their faces. We've got some, like Josh there, who are just plain scared. Others, like Joe O'Hara, are too eager. The one thing or the other can get you killed."

"Josh and I are as old as George," I reminded him.

"And George is in the hands of the enemy now," he reminded me. "Maybe riding with Ferguson or Tarleton, for all we know. His brothers are dead. And for what?"

The question hung hauntingly in the air, unanswered.

We remained in camp until October 4. All that time, we were complaining. If we were going to fight Ferguson, we should do it. The newest rumor had Dragging Canoe back on the march. We had come to protect our families, not leave them unguarded against old enemies.

The question of command was finally settled when Col. Charles McDowell, who probably should have been in charge, volunteered to carry a letter to General Gates over in Hillsborough. In his place, Col. William Campbell, who commanded a Virginia regiment, would take the army in hand. Colonel Campbell was famous for driving Tories out of Virginia and punishing others in varying parts of the Carolinas. He was downright huge! Joe said it seemed an unfair burden for a horse to carry a man that big.

Colonel Campbell wasted no time in gathering us together.

"The enemy is at hand," he shouted. We had to fight him. We were to perform a great service for our country, something our sons would boast about. He finally offered any man who chose the chance to leave.

The other colonels, and even Maj. Joe McDowell, then spoke of the shame that would fall on any man who left. Col. Isaac Shelby suggested that anyone choosing to avoid the fighting step back from his comrades. No one moved. A roar rose from the ranks. We cheered our fellow soldiers. Pa gripped my shoulders, and I thought I detected a tear in his eye. We formed into our different commands and headed south. Finally, we were on the way to Gilbert Town.

Our delay had allowed the Tories to escape. Gilbert Town was nearly deserted. Ferguson had marched away, leaving little of value behind. The patriot families cheered our return, but I could read some bitterness on the faces of women who had seemingly been left to the wolves when their husbands marched off into the mountains.

Colonel Campbell dispatched scouts, mainly local men, into the surrounding country.

"I'd still like to have some pictures of the enemy camps," Major McDowell told me. "Will you ride ahead again, Francis?"

"He's staying with us," Pa declared. "Wherever Ferguson will be, he won't still be there when it's time to fight."

I could tell the major was disappointed, but what Pa said made sense.

"So, we're going to be ordinary soldiers, eh?" Joe asked.

"Disappointed?" Pa asked.

"No," Joe declared. "I don't figure you need scouts who don't know the country. Pretty soon only our rifles will matter."

That same day two South Carolina scouts rode right into Ferguson's camp. In fact, they captured his cook! They then sat down, ate the major's breakfast, and learned the Tory army was headed south. All the old worries about Tarleton and Cornwallis returned. We passed burned cabins and learned of murdered patriots. The army's mood turned gloomy. I began to worry about Ma, Kate, and my brothers.

All that changed when we came across Ferguson's proclamation. Copies were nailed to trees and buildings throughout the countryside. Once the major's words got around, people grew angry.

Some said he was trying to scare the mountain Tories into joining his command. Some insisted that he was trying to scare the mountain people into abandoning the rebellion. I don't suppose anybody except the major knew for certain why he had issued his proclamation. It was what kept our army together, though.

It was pure fiction, the notion that we were the ones

doing all the burning and murdering!

"We all know who's been doing that," I said angrily.

"He's not warning anybody," Joe said. "He's threatening us with the same treatment he and Tarleton and every Tory in the Carolinas have been handing out! He's inviting us to our own hangings! Well, no Watauga man ever sat around waiting for war to come to his doorstep!"

Joe spoke for the whole army. None of us was a bit less afraid. But we were mad, and we figured coming all that way from home, we might as well see the job done.

Ferguson didn't head south for long. He turned east, toward the safety of Cornwallis's army at Charlotte. We were mostly mounted, and by October 5, we were just a day behind Ferguson. He passed that night camped among friendly Tories near a broad meadow known as Hannah's Cowpens. The following morning we were up with the sun. There was little doubt we would soon be facing the enemy.

The colonels were faced with some hard choices that morning. A courier was captured with letters from Ferguson to Cornwallis, requesting reinforcement. Tarleton's cavalry was rumored to be no more than two days away. We had to strike swiftly or lose our chance. Colonel Campbell ordered all men without good horses to follow afoot. Those of us with good mounts would hurry ahead.

It was a hard thing for those left behind. Some of the older and younger soldiers gave up their mounts to better-armed or more experienced soldiers. Mr. Moore turned

Josh's black mare over to a scarred Virginia corporal.

"Son, maybe you and Josh should both follow the main body," Pa told me. "You're young and better able to walk."

"I've come this far," I answered. "It's too late to turn the work over to others."

"You can't imagine what's coming," Pa argued. "Do you know, son, that I once went into battle beside my father?"

"No, sir," I answered.

"You've surely heard of Culloden Moor, though."

"That's where the Highland Scots lost to King George," I said, recalling Grandma's old story of the bloody killing of the Highlanders, how my grandpa and two of my uncles lost their lives at the sharp points of English bayonets.

"In those days, every man of any size rallied to his kinsmen. We left our homes and families to restore King James to his rightful throne. His own son, Prince Charles, led us south, almost to London. But the prince was inclined to celebrate victories never won, and we ended up retreating almost to Inverness. The English and their Lowland friends were waiting for us there, in a bog. It wasn't ground favorable to our cause, but the prince bid us do his fighting there. Our charge was courageous, and our cries split the heavens. We died in our hundreds, shot by English muskets and stabbed by English bayonets. I was fourteen at the time, same as you are now. I hid in tall grass for hours as the English moved among the dead, stripping the bodies and carrying away our swords and pistols."

"They found you?"

"Toward nightfall, I set off to locate my father. He was shot to pieces. My brothers were nearby, their bellies opened by bayonets. They caught me sitting there, in tears. A sergeant wanted to cut me down, but an officer happened along and ordered me taken to a hut. Outside, they argued over what to do with us. Some prisoners were to be sent to London, it seemed, but there were too many of us. Two huts were set afire. I was lucky, I suppose. Our hut wasn't set afire. I still hear the screams of my dying cousins and neighbors in my dreams!

"Francis, you carry the name of my eldest brother, struck down three weeks short of his eighteenth birthday. I spent a year in an English prison ship and five more years in bondage in the Carolinas before your grandmother located me and purchased my liberty. Every day and night for six years, I swore that no son of mine would know bondage. And I swore the day would never arise when a boy child of mine would have to fight his people's battles."

"You never told me any of this, Pa."

"I suppose I believed if no one knew, it could never happen. But I've two dead nephews and possibly a third. My oldest boy's in his grave, and now I've brought you here."

"I brought myself," I told him.

"We're here, the both of us, in any case. But there's no need we both continue. You've done enough already, Francis. No one will think less of you if you join Josh."

"You wouldn't?"

"I'd be glad of it, son."

"Then I suppose it's only for myself that I'm going. Maybe so there won't be any English bayonets around when my sons are fourteen."

"I can't say I'm not proud of you, Francis," he said, pulling me to his side. "But I'd rather you be safe."

I tried to smile. Pa nodded grimly, and we climbed atop our horses.

Altogether, there were seven hundred of us in the advance party. We probably weren't equal to the task of defeating Ferguson, but we were capable of cutting off his retreat. The others could join us in time for the battle.

I suppose everything about that day was odd. We rode out less like a single army than as several mobs of neighbors. Colonel Campbell remained in charge of his Virginians, and the other colonels led their detachments. No one seemed to have a clear notion of where we were headed, but all of us nevertheless reached the Cowpens about the same time that evening. Hannah, who had built the enclosure, had left years before. That October a Tory named Hiram Saunders owned the place, and he refused even to open his door.

I heard later that his wife announced that her husband was ill and in bed. Some of our men burst inside, though, dragged Saunders from his bed, and questioned him about Ferguson. The Tory provided no answers, even when terrible threats were issued. Matt Lewis even threw one end of a rope over the limb of a large oak.

"I cannot tell you what I don't know," Saunders declared.

In the end, it didn't matter. We had another source of information. Two of our scouts arrived with a strange, ragged-looking old man. Josiah Fairweather dismounted his horse and made an exaggerated bow.

"Well, gentlemen, shall we discuss Pat Ferguson's funeral?" he asked.

I couldn't help laughing.

While some of our soldiers slaughtered Tory cows and others cooked a supper of beefsteak and corn bread, our spy told the colonels how he had befriended the area Tories and pried from them the needed information. Ferguson was only hours away, camped atop a low ridge known as Kings Mountain. The major had with him over a thousand men. Six hundred Tories were on their way to join him. Cornwallis had not left Charlotte, but there was no word of Tarleton. Even at full gallop, though, he was more than a day away. If we hurried, we could deal with Ferguson before help arrived. Then we could turn on his six hundred recruits and speed them homeward.

I might never have learned all this had not our old friend Mr. Fairweather spotted Joe and me chewing beef beside our campfire. He greeted us as lost nephews, and we invited him to share our supper.

"So you've made your choice," he told me. "It's a fine thing you young men are going to do. Some of us are too old for the fighting and have to serve in other ways."

"We've been scouting most of the time," Joe told the old man. "We've had our close calls."

"Spying is a game that requires an old man's cunning,"

Mr. Fairweather told us. "Young men don't have the patience to do it right."

I nodded. Spending weeks and months among the enemy, pretending friendship, just on the chance that you might aid your friends, was beyond my abilities. In Camden I hadn't even been able to stay out of trouble a few days!

We set off for Kings Mountain after eating. I rode between Pa and Joe, but none of us spoke a word. It began raining, and a chill wind tormented us.

"Cover your rifle," Pa told me. "Never mind that you're nearly frozen and wet through to the bone. A soldier's nothing without dry powder and a reliable rifle."

Other veterans of Indian fights and clashes with the Tories and British also instructed their companions. Soon we rode half-naked through the hills. I shivered from head to toe, and I felt ice forming on my eyebrows. I had never been so miserable.

I became almost numb as we continued. There was a brief pause when we reached the Broad River. It was the perfect place for an ambush, and scouts forded the stream and patrolled the far bank. Ferguson's men were apparently in their camp, under the cover of their tents. We crossed the river and rode on.

Clouds had swallowed the moon, and it was entirely dark. I guided my horse more by sound than anything else. During this time Colonel Campbell and his four hundred Virginians got lost, and for a while our detachment was pitifully weak. In time the lost men were found, though, and we were again an army.

I was dead on my feet by then. Once, I almost fell out of the saddle. Pa moved over and began singing one of his old Scottish tunes. I took up the melody on my mouth organ, and we both returned to life for a time. Colonel Campbell suggested stopping to rest, but I think it was Colonel Shelby who shouted that he intended to keep going until he met Ferguson or Cornwallis, one or the other.

We were still riding when the sun finally broke through the clouds that next morning. The rain stopped, and I shook some of the weariness from my soul. As I glanced around at my companions, I saw only pale, freezing men and boys, all of them near the end of their tether.

We soon came upon a cabin. A defiant Tory rushed out and glared at us.

"You'll soon meet your end!" he told us.

His daughter offered us a sly smile.

"Where's Ferguson?" someone asked her.

"Atop yon mountain," she answered. She pointed to a rocky, tree-covered ridge just ahead.

"Kings Mountain," one of the South Carolinians declared.

Kings Mountain

10

E RODE ANOTHER FIVE miles before halting near the base of Kings Mountain. All of us knew what was waiting on that stony ridge. We dismounted and tried our best to wring the water from our shirts and coats. Mostly, though, we attended to our rifles.

Pa busied himself overseeing my preparations.

"I hadn't noticed your shoulders broadening so," he said as he helped me wriggle into my soggy shirt. "You've gone and grown tall on me, Francis."

"Not so tall," I said, shaking my head. "I've got a ways to go yet."

"Not by my reckoning," he declared. "Today it benefits a man not to be too tall. The smaller a man is, the harder it is to hit him!"

"Is it hard, Pa?" I asked.

"What?"

"Shooting a man," I said, shuddering. "Killing a man."

"Most difficult thing there is," he told me. "The day it

comes easy, though, is the day you'll wish you hadn't been born. A man fights and kills because he has to. He protects those who can't protect themselves. He looks after his home and family. It's always been that way, Francis. It always will be."

"Don't those people on that mountain feel the same way?" I asked.

"Probably," Pa said, nodding soberly. "If they didn't, our job wouldn't be so hard. You remember when Old Abram's men attacked Fort Caswell? Why, every young man who charged our wall put me in mind of your ma's cousins. Today you'll see men who look no different from you or me. But when they raise their rifles or point their bayonets, they'll be your enemy. You'll shoot them because it's the way of things. Or you'll let them shoot you or one of your friends. Understand?"

"I hope so, Pa. But I'm not sure."

"A lot of boys gathered here won't say so, but they likely share the feeling. Or they're too scared to have considered it."

I nodded. By then, the colonels had finished planning the fight. One column after another set off to take their positions. Colonel Sevier had been chosen to attack the far western end of the mountain. Because we had the shortest distance to march, we left last. Colonel Shelby's men would be on our left. Colonel Campbell placed his Virginians on our right. He would attack Ferguson's center from the south. The main Tory camp stood on the eastern hump of the ridge, where a good spring provided water. I expected the hardest fighting to be there. I didn't mind that we were as far from that point as possible.

Once Colonel Sevier gave the order to advance, I took a deep breath and followed Pa. Joe O'Hara was at my side. He had his rifle in hand and a big hunting knife rested in

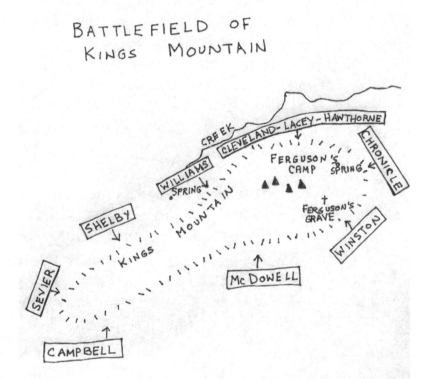

BATTLEFIELD OF
KINGS MOUNTAIN

a sheath on his left hip. Always before, Joe had appeared so much older and more confident than I was. That afternoon he seemed to be lost and very alone.

When we reached our assigned position, we calmly loaded our rifles and waited for the order to advance. When it didn't come, I turned my attention to the mountain itself. Kings Mountain was a little less than half a mile long. From the base to the summit, thick trees and heavy brush covered every inch of the slope. The crown was bare, making a fine campground for a thousand men. But it was a poor place to defend. Our men had good cover while the defenders would be in the open. We were also able to shoot upward without endangering the soldiers attacking up the opposite slope. The Tories, on the other hand, would be hemmed in and caught in a crossfire. They were mostly farmers from the lowlands and less at home in the woods. Ferguson had drilled them to line up and fire in volleys. That tactic had won the battle at Camden. It stood a poor chance of discouraging crack riflemen concealed behind rocks and trees.

I couldn't help but marvel at the sight of the place that afternoon. The leaves had begun to turn, and splashes of orange and yellow and red clashed with the bright blue of a clearing sky. Dressed in our buckskins, we crept upon the enemy like shadows. We took cover and waited. When Colonel Sevier ordered us forward, Pa grabbed my arm.

"Whatever you do, stay on my right and keep under cover," he said. "If you have to be here, for God's sake do as I say."

"It's not the worst place I can think of to be," I replied. "I'd hate to be facing this alone."

My eyes were on Joe. Pa noticed. He stepped over and grabbed Joe O'Hara.

"Whatever you do, son, stay on my left," he told Joe.

"Sir?" Joe asked, clearly surprised.

"We're all of us kinsmen today," he said, glancing over at me. "Nobody's alone."

I had little chance to consider what Pa had said. At that instant, the sound of drumming filled the air. Shouts of alarm carried across the mountain. Muskets erupted just ahead and along the side of the ridge. I heard a shrill whistle and cries of "Form up." Our approach had been discovered. It was around three o'clock. The battle had begun.

Pa had said that none of us was alone, but once the fighting started, I sure felt that way. Some of the more experienced men rushed ahead while a lot of the boys hung back. I did my best to stay alongside Pa, but a big maple tree blocked our path. I went right as Pa went left. I lost sight of him.

From what I could tell, we got maybe halfway up the side of the mountain before the Tories fired their first volley. There were about a hundred of them in line, and they shot their muskets on command. A sheet of flame nearly blinded me. Lead balls tore leaves and splintered branches on the trees overhead. The Tories then gave a cry and started toward us with their bayonets. The trees and rocks broke their line, but they continued in twos and threes. I heard a scream and froze. Then just ahead, a tall, heavyset man with a big British musket appeared. A twig snapped to my left, and I saw Joe take aim and fire. His shot went wide. The Tory started toward Joe. As the man took his third step, I raised my rifle, rammed back the hammer, and fired. There was a moment's delay as the flint sparked the powder. Then the louder report of the powder igniting sent a lead ball flying through the air. It struck the Tory's right shoulder, spinning him around. Before he could recover from the shock, two other shots struck him in the chest and forehead, killing him.

"Joe, are you hurt?" I called.

He dropped to his knees beside a boulder. His face was pale as death. I raced over and searched for signs of a wound. I found none.

"No holes in you," I assured him.

"Guess not," he said, struggling to his feet. "You saved my life."

"I only distracted him," I said, steadying my trembling hands. "Some fellows on our right did the killing."

"Francis, I think I'll stay here a minute and catch my breath," Joe announced.

"I'd better find Pa," I told him. "Join us later."

I headed up the ridge, but a group of green-shirted men were on their way down. They kept their line in good order despite the thick forest, and our boys turned and fled. I saw Pa twenty feet to my left and darted in that direction. He took aim and dropped one of the attacking Tories. I raised my rifle, but before I could cock the hammer, I realized I hadn't reloaded. I turned and raced after Pa. We stopped together at the base of the mountain and reloaded.

"It's not what I expected," I declared.

"Never is," he said as he rammed a ball down his barrel. "I thought you'd be on my right."

"Got lost for a time," I explained.

He grinned. Once I reloaded my rifle, we charged back up the slope together. This time maybe twenty of us fired at the line of green shirts. Four of them fell. Two more were cut down by rifle fire from the far left. The others swept us from the ridge with their bayonets, though.

We finally got up the mountain on our fourth try. Half of Colonel Shelby's men were already there. I later learned that the men in green shirts were Ferguson's American Rangers, the best soldiers in his army. We killed fifteen of them before they fled.

The fighting then became pretty confused. With men from so many different commands atop Kings Mountain, it was hard to tell friend from foe. Most of the Tories had retreated to their camp on the opposite end of the ridge. The rest were scattered about in little pockets of four or five, fighting for their lives.

I stayed with Pa. We slowly made our way east along the crest. He stopped and inspected each fallen body. Most were dead, but occasionally he would find a wounded man or even one who was unhurt and merely feigning death.

"This one's plenty alive," Pa announced, gripping the Tory by his shirt and dragging him to his feet.

"Give him to me," a familiar voice shouted. I turned and saw Matt Lewis stomping toward us.

"He's a prisoner," I objected.

"He's one of the ones who was bragging about hanging my brother," Matt growled. "I remember him from Gilbert Town."

"That right?" Pa asked the Tory.

"You're mistaken," the Tory insisted. "I have a cousin who looks just like me. Maybe he was the one. I never hanged anybody in my life."

Matt grabbed the man by his hair and slammed him against a tree. He then tore the man's coat off and pointed out his embroidered shirt.

"My brother's," Matt explained.

"I'm a prisoner!" the Tory shouted. "I'm unarmed!"

"My brother wasn't armed, either," Matt replied as he dragged the man away. "He was fifteen!"

Pa gripped my arm and led me away. There was still fighting up ahead, and we went that way.

I don't know how many Tories came across relatives of their victims. There was a lot of bad blood between some of the South Carolina militia and the Tories in Ferguson's command. I heard quite a few of the enemy were killed after they tried to surrender. There was shooting going on elsewhere, and nobody could be sure what was happening. But when a Tory was found with a friend's watch or a father's ring, he rarely saw another sunrise.

Joe O'Hara reappeared then. He accompanied Pa and me as we made our way among the rocks, rooting out Tories. Just ahead, three men arose from the rocks and discharged their rifles. Two shots hit on our right, but the third whistled past my left ear. Pa shoved me to the ground. When a fourth Tory rose, Joe shot him through the head. Pa hit a second man in the right knee. The others tossed out their muskets and pleaded for their lives.

"Come out slowly," Pa demanded.

Two stepped out with arms raised. Their eyes were full of terror. The wounded Tory limped along after them. Joe and I collected their muskets. I caught sight of a fifth man in the rocks and turned my rifle toward him.

"Come out, now!" I shouted.

He rose slowly, cradling his left arm. He limped badly, and I thought he might have suffered a second wound.

Even though he tried to hide his face, there was something very familiar about him.

"George?" I asked.

"Francis," he answered.

Hurt and frightened as he was, George turned and hobbled toward me. I caught him in my arms as he stumbled. We both fell to the ground.

"You're hurt," I said, examining his leg.

"Twisted my ankle," he explained. "But somebody put a ball through my arm."

I took a deep breath and let it out. Then I pried his fingers from the bloody mess that was his left forearm.

"Let me," Pa said. He dipped a strip of cloth in water and began washing the wound. "You're a lucky boy, George," Pa observed. "Ball went through the flesh. Missed the bone."

"You know me, sir?" George asked.

"This is my pa," I told him. "Your uncle John."

"Then I suppose we're both lucky," George said, wincing as Pa began binding the wound. "I'm alive, and you've still got a pa."

"I guess things look a little better than the last time we were together," I admitted.

"Maybe," George said, eyeing the others. "What's going to happen to me now? I heard some men shouting 'Tarleton's quarter.' You don't mean to shoot us all, do you?"

"You've already been shot once," I told him.

"A second shot would be a waste of lead," Pa added. "Your ma will be glad you're safe."

"Am I safe?" George asked nervously.

"You are," I assured him.

Not everyone was, though. The fighting continued on the western end of the ridge for another quarter hour. I learned later that Ferguson and his Rangers rushed from point to point, rallying the other Tories and fending off attacks. It was his whistle I had heard. It attracted plenty of attention. The major was riding a tall horse and made a good target, too. When he led his men in a desperate attempt to break our line, a dozen rifles marked him as their target. Joe O'Hara told me he saw Ferguson's body. There were at least eight balls in it.

Ferguson's second in command, Capt. Abraham De Peyster, continued the fight for a time. It was hopeless, though. He finally surrendered what remained of Ferguson's army. Altogether, more than 200 Tories were dead. Another 150 were wounded. The remaining 700 huddled in a circle, prisoners of Virginia and Carolina militia and overmountain men. Of our own soldiers, 28 were dead. Another 62 had been wounded.

By the time the powder smoke lifted, I managed to locate most of my friends and neighbors. Fortunately, none of them had any holes in them. I learned later that Matt Lewis had charged three Tories and been shot through the heart.

"Maybe it was for the best," his cousin Amos said. "He wasn't the same man after we left Gilbert Town."

I agreed that the lieutenant had changed. So had I, though. I prayed I would never lose my senses the way that Matt had.

With the battle won and Ferguson dead, much still

remained to be done. Daylight was fading, and more than two hundred dead men lay scattered atop the mountain. The six hundred Tories who had been on their way to join Ferguson were probably nearby, and Cornwallis with his thousands of veteran regulars was less than forty miles away at Charlotte.

We had been a day and a half riding hard and fighting a battle, though. Once we had collected all of the Tories' weapons, a guard was posted to watch the prisoners. We then spread our blankets on the mountain. Pa found us a flat space under a sheltering oak. George and I slept on either side of him. Joe O'Hara lay at our feet.

"Some nights it feels especially good to be alive," Pa told me as I wrapped myself in a warm blanket liberated from the Tory camp.

"I think every night's going to be that way from now on," I replied.

"Will for me," George added.

"And me," Joe said. "It was a close thing, too. I thought they had us when they charged with their bayonets."

I disagreed. Tories armed with English steel were one thing. We were armed with the sword of the Lord and of Gideon. If you relied on divine providence as I did, then the outcome had never been in doubt.

11

ORNING FOUND US COLD and hungry. We expected to find a hoard of food and ammunitions in Ferguson's camp. There was almost nothing to eat. By the time the Tories surrendered, they had exhausted their supply of shot and powder. I had only three rifle balls left. Pa had four. Joe was completely out. It was the same throughout the army.

The only things we had in great supply were British muskets—and prisoners. We had seven hundred Tories and more than twelve hundred extra guns. Strange as it seemed, our solution to the problem of transporting the captured weapons was to have the prisoners carry them. Naturally, each musket had been unloaded.

Everyone in the patriot army was eager to leave Kings Mountain. We needed to find food, and half the men expected Tarleton's cavalry to appear at any moment. The colonels met to decide what to do. In the end, Colonel Campbell's Virginians remained to deal with the wounded and bury the dead. Relatives chose to carry some men's bodies homeward. We buried the rest of our dead in a single pit. The Tories were buried in a second pit. Major Ferguson was placed in a shallow trench by one of his soldiers. Others piled rocks over the spot, erecting a cairn like the one I had helped build at Camden.

Only the wounded well enough to walk or ride accompanied us. We left the Tories at neighboring farms. Our own gravely wounded usually chose to return northward with the army. Some died along the way and were buried beside the road. The others recovered.

The prisoners posed a serious problem. There were not enough of us to provide an adequate guard, and escapes became common. A number of the captured Tories, like George, had friends and relatives among our men. They didn't remain captives long. Colonel Shelby freed dozens of prisoners who had previously served in his command. They claimed that Ferguson had threatened to burn their homes had they not joined his army. Others said their choice had been death. No one who had heard of the killings and hangings doubted that it was the truth.

As we retraced our steps north, we found little to eat. Once we dug up a field of sweet potatoes. Another time we survived on roasted pumpkins. When we approached Gilbert Town three days after the battle, some of our men began killing farm animals and stealing corn from the cribs. Our hungry men raided friend and foe alike, and Colonel Campbell scolded us for ignoring the rights of our friends.

"Best thing to do is go home," Pa argued. It was the common feeling of all the Watauga men. But we had hundreds of prisoners. We couldn't just release them. Many of the South Carolina men wanted to hang them all. Others argued that anyone willing to sign a pledge not to serve against us in the future should be allowed to leave. In the end, a trial was held, and each case was considered in turn. The judges sentenced thirty-six to be hanged. Nine were actually executed before the younger brother of the tenth cut his bonds and assisted his escape. The hangings were conducted in the early hours of the morning, and only a few of our soldiers had remained awake to witness the scene. They didn't have the heart to continue, so the remaining condemned prisoners were spared.

Perhaps it was for the best. One grateful survivor told Colonel Shelby that the dreaded Tarleton was due to attack our camp at dawn. The colonels roused us early, and we posted a heavy rear guard. Soon the entire army was hurrying northward. In spite of a cold, driving rain, we covered over thirty miles that day. Only when safely on the far side of the swollen Catawba River did anyone relax. The rising river would afford us protection even if Tarleton did appear. During our frantic march, a hundred Tories escaped. When we learned later that Tarleton and Cornwallis, fearing an attack by ten thousand mountain men, were hurrying south, we could only laugh.

I remained with the army just one more day. Major McDowell invited me to dinner at his house, and Pa argued that I would be ungrateful not to accept. In return, I drew a sketch of the major. Due to lack of rest and nourishment, it wasn't my best work. Nevertheless, Major McDowell deemed it a good likeness and fed me all the roast pork, boiled potatoes, and fresh greens I could eat.

"I hope we have the opportunity to serve together again," the major told me when he led the way outside after dinner. "Our nation has need of young men like you."

"Thank you for saying so, sir," I replied. "But I don't know that I've got any more soldiering in me. I mainly want to go home and see my ma."

"No man living can find fault with such sentiments," he said. "God bless you, Francis."

"And you, sir," I answered.

Messengers had arrived with reports that the Cherokees were preparing a winter attack on the Watauga valley settlements, and Colonel Sevier assembled most of his own and Colonel Shelby's men. We were to return to the mountains and prevent such a raid.

So it was that we left the prisoners to our fellow soldiers and returned home. Ten days after destroying Ferguson's army at Kings Mountain, I knocked on the door of my cabin. Kate opened the door. Smiling brightly, she wrapped her arms around me and nearly accomplished what a thousand Tories had been unable to do—suffocate me. If possible, she gave an even warmer greeting to George. Pa told us later that he felt like he'd been reduced to playing third fiddle. Ma greeted him with a hundred kisses, though, and my brothers swarmed around him like crazed bees.

In December Pa set off with Colonel Sevier to fight

Dragging Canoe again. I stayed home.

"You've done your fighting," Pa declared. "Look after your family."

This time I saw no disappointment in his eyes. I saw instead the love and encouragement Ma had always offered.

That afternoon snow began falling. Jamie and Alek raced outside and began their private snowball war. Ma laughed at them. Kate was spinning wool into yarn. I glanced at the woodpile and grabbed Pa's ax, then walked out and began splitting logs.

I paused and watched my brothers a moment. It was funny how things had changed those past few months. Before, I would have sat beside the fire, drawing and waiting for Ma to tell me what needed doing. Or perhaps I would have wrestled with Jamie and Alek in the snow. But I was no longer a child. I'd accepted a man's responsibilities. And if I was neither as tall nor as wise and capable as Pa, I knew the time for being idle and irresponsible was gone. After Camden and Kings Mountain, there was no going back. I picked up the ax and continued chopping.

Author's Note

*I*N 1962, WHEN I WAS just a schoolboy, my uncle Bob Wisler gave me a two-volume history of the American Revolution. Years later, after exploring sites from Lexington and Fort Ticonderoga to Saratoga and Yorktown, I thought I had a sense of how the war had been fought and won.

"You need to go to Kings Mountain," he told me.

It never seemed to be on the way to anything, though, and besides, my history books mentioned the fight there as a skirmish, something of scant importance. How wrong they were! As I read and analyzed the events of 1780, I was convinced that the road to victory started at Kings Mountain.

Historical fiction is always a tightrope act. Authors must balance the twin tasks of incorporating facts and telling a story. I chose for my voice Francis Livingstone, a boy like many who yearn for independence from home and family, yet cling to both in times of trial. His family and neighbors are inventions based on my research of the Watauga people and community.

Many actual historical figures walk these pages. There was a Banastre Tarleton, a Patrick Ferguson, and a Charles

Cornwallis. Captain Jarvis is a representation of many Tory commanders. Among the patriots, I have featured many of the key players—the McDowell brothers, the Reverend Samuel Doak, Colonels Sevier and Shelby, etcetera. I have relied on their own words, whenever possible, and the recollections of others when not. The events depicted within these pages are as accurate as I could make them. If patriot and Tory do not always seem consistently good or evil, it is because few people are.

I hope that my readers will enjoy Francis's story but also gain a glimpse into a too-long-neglected chapter in America's struggle for independence. I have provided sketches and maps to help clarify the story. I hope you enjoy this brief journey through our nation's past.

G. *Clifton Wisler*
Plano, Texas

The American Revolution in the South

NUMBER OF HISTORIANS HAVE referred to the Civil War (1861–1865) as the Second American Revolution. Perhaps, though, in discussing the American Revolution in the South, it would be more accurate to call the conflict America's First Civil War. While British armies did participate, Americans did most of the fighting, suffering, and dying. Those who favored independence called themselves patriots. The British considered them rebels. Americans loyal to King George III called themselves Tories, and they were numerous in the South. Families were split, and neighbors often chose opposing sides. The war was vicious. Both sides burned homes, stole livestock, and murdered their enemies.

In the beginning, though, the South seemed securely in the hands of the rebellious Americans. An early effort to rally loyal Scots in North Carolina was crushed at Moore's Creek Bridge in February 1776. And when the British struck at Charleston, South Carolina, in June of that same year, a mixed force of militia (volunteers who enlisted for a few weeks or months) and Continentals (trained state soldiers enlisted for longer terms) drove off a powerful fleet of warships. Patriot forces controlled the South the following two years while the British army fought in the North.

When British regulars landed near Savannah, Georgia, on December 23, 1778, the war in the South took a dramatic turn. Georgia militia and a small force of Continentals rushed to defend the key port, but they were overwhelmed on December 29. Of approximately one thousand American defenders, nearly one hundred were killed or captured. Another five hundred were taken prisoner. The survivors fled into the nearby swamps.

To deal with the British invasion, Congress dispatched southward a Massachusetts general, Benjamin Lincoln. Lincoln failed to recapture Savannah despite aid from the French. He then retreated to Charleston. Tories who had hidden their true feelings eagerly rallied to the British flag. Patriot leaders had their homes burned, property stolen, and livestock slaughtered. Many people who sided with the rebellion signed loyalty oaths to the king. Georgia, to a great extent, was lost to the patriot cause.

South Carolina was the next colony to suffer invasion. First, British and Tory soldiers struck north from Georgia. Lincoln asked for and received the veteran southern Continentals who had gone north to serve in Gen. George Washington's army. With a force of several thousand soldiers, most of them trained and determined to fight, he was in a position to defend the state. Instead, he was trapped inside the city of Charleston when a large British army under the command of Sir Henry Clinton landed on the coast on March 29, 1780, and surrounded the city. On May 12, Lincoln surrendered his army. His defeat eliminated the only organized American army in the South.

Clinton sailed north, leaving the command of the southern British armies in the hands of Gen. Charles Cornwallis. Aided ably by a Scottish major, Patrick Ferguson, and a young English cavalryman, Col. Banastre Tarleton, Cornwallis began establishing garrisons across the state.

In one of the most vicious events of the war, Tarleton attacked a group of retreating Virginia militia commanded by Col. Abraham Buford in the Waxhaws country near the border between North and South Carolina. Tarleton massacred all prisoners, giving birth to the term "Tarleton's quarter." It was a signal that the war in the Carolinas would be a campaign without mercy.

Other than small forces of militia and the defiant forces of Francis Marion and Thomas Sumter, who raided British outposts and terrorized South Carolina Tories, Cornwallis was unopposed. Congress ordered Gen. Horatio Gates, the victorious commander of American forces at Saratoga, to go south with the Delaware and Maryland Continentals. Reinforced by Gen. Richard Caswell's North Carolina militia and smaller detachments scattered across the South, Gates marched on Cornwallis's main force and attacked them at Camden on August 16, 1780. In one of the most decisive battles of the war, Gates was thoroughly defeated. Those soldiers in his command not killed or captured fled in every direction.

As if things weren't bad enough for the American cause, Cornwallis sent Ferguson and Tarleton westward, killing and burning. Tarleton added to his reputation when he struck Sumter's command on August 18, routing the militia entirely. It was Ferguson's march westward, toward the mountains, and his proclamation to lay waste to all rebel strongholds, that rallied the patriot militia and angered the overmountain men along the Watauga. Inspired by the Reverend Samuel Doak and determined to drive Ferguson from their doorstep, the men took up arms and chased Ferguson to Kings Mountain where, on October 7, 1780, they destroyed the Tory army, killed Ferguson, and dramatically changed the course of American history.

The startling destruction of Ferguson's army so close to Cornwallis's base at Charlotte, North Carolina, shattered British plans and eroded their confidence. Then, when Tarleton's legion, supported by British regulars, met defeat in January 1781 at the Battle of Cowpens, Cornwallis's plans lay in shambles.

The dual victories inspired American patriots and led many Tories to turn away from the king's cause. When George Washington sent Nathaniel Greene, a competent general, to take command in the South, British hopes grew dimmer still. He never defeated Cornwallis on the battle-field. But Greene's ability to evade destruction while inflicting critical losses on his British adversary forced Cornwallis to retreat first to a base at Wilmington, North Carolina, and then to the Virginia peninsula. There, at Yorktown on October 19, 1781, a little more than a year after the battle of Kings Mountain, the British army in the South marched out and stacked its arms. Although a peace treaty was not signed until 1783, and large British forces remained in New York, the British government understood the significance of Cornwallis's defeat. The American colonies had become a new nation.

Chronology of Key Events

February 27, 1776

North Carolina militia defeat loyalists at Moore's Creek Bridge, near Wilmington, North Carolina.

June 28, 1776

Patriots at Sullivans Island defeat a British fleet, saving Charleston from invasion.

July 4, 1776

Delegates from the American colonies issue a Declaration of Independence.

July 20, 1776

Watauga militia defeat the Cherokees at Island Flats.

December 29, 1778

British forces capture Savannah, Georgia, driving off Georgia militia and a small force of Continentals.

October 9, 1779

American and French attack fails to recapture Savannah.

March 29, 1780

Sir Henry Clinton lands near Charleston, South Carolina, with a major British army.

May 12, 1780

Gen. Benjamin Lincoln surrenders Charleston and the only large American army in the South.

May 29, 1780

Col. Banastre Tarleton massacres Virginia militia under Col. Abraham Buford at the Waxhaws, near the North Carolina–South Carolina border.

August 16, 1780

Gen. Charles Cornwallis destroys Gen. Horatio Gates's patriot army at Camden.

October 7, 1780

Patriot militia defeats Maj. Patrick Ferguson's Tory army at Kings Mountain.

January 17, 1781

Daniel Morgan leads a mixed force of Continentals and militia to defeat Tarleton at the Battle of Cowpens (South Carolina).

March 15, 1781

Cornwallis defeats the patriot army of Gen. Nathaniel Greene at the Battle of Guildford Courthouse (North Carolina). Cornwallis is forced to retreat toward Wilmington, North Carolina.

October 19, 1781

Cornwallis surrenders to Gen. George Washington at Yorktown, Virginia.

Acknowledgments

O N OCTOBER 7, 1999, on a chilly, rainy day, I stood on the slopes of Kings Mountain on the North Carolina–South Carolina border. I wondered how it must have felt to a fourteen-year-old soldier in the patriot army standing on that same ground 219 years earlier, facing the dreaded army of Maj. Patrick Ferguson and his army of American loyalists. My arrival at Kings Mountain marked the completion of a ten-day journey from Elizabethton, Tennessee, following in the steps of the overmountain men on what has become the Overmountain Victory Trail. Along the way, I enjoyed the friendship and assistance of numerous local historians, as well as the staffs at Sycamore Shoals State Park in Tennessee and Cowpens National Battlefield and Kings Mountain National Military Park in South Carolina.* I was especially fortunate to pass my afternoon at Kings Mountain with living historians—teachers, firefighters, police officers, and even schoolchildren—who devote their spare time to making the past come alive. It's amazing

*I have used the nonpossessive spelling, Kings Mountain, throughout. The site was named after early settlers, the Kings.

how much one can learn when the rain keeps everyone else away.

In addition to using primary-source material such as Revolutionary War pension applications and after-battle reports, I relied heavily on Lyman Draper's classic work, *King's Mountain and Its Heroes,* as well as Hank Messick's more recent work, *King's Mountain.* I received a great deal of help from the friendly volunteers at Historic Camden, South Carolina, who allowed me to roam their restored village at will, answered dozens of questions, and helped me locate and understand the scenes of conflict in Kershaw County. The model for the White Stag Tavern is located at Ninety-six National Historic Site in South Carolina.

I have grown to rely on the research facilities of the Central Branch of the Dallas Public Library. I feel fortunate to live so close to this outstanding facility, where all visitors are treated like friends and neighbors. If there is a better place to dig into America's past, I haven't discovered it. I appreciate the assistance of volunteers at the genealogical collection of the Gladys Harrington Public Library in my hometown of Plano, Texas. I am equally grateful to the interlibrary loan librarians, who always seem capable of locating and delivering old, obscure volumes needed in my research. Finally, I must acknowledge the fine collections of the University of North Texas, where I have learned the process of conducting historical research.